Look for More Titles by Cassandra Chandler

The Krampus

Court of the Yuletide Fae
Book Three

Cassandra Chandler

Copyright Page

This book is pure fiction. All characters, places, names, and events are products of the author's imagination or used solely in a fictitious manner. Any resemblance to any people, places, things, or events that have ever existed or will ever exist is entirely coincidental.

The Krampus
Court of the Yuletide Fae, Book Three
Copyright © 2023 by Cassandra Chandler
Print ISBN: 978-1-945702-17-4
Digital ISBN: 978-1-945702-16-7

First eBook edition: February 2023
First print edition: February 2023
10 9 8 7 6 5 4 3 2 1

cassandra-chandler.com
P.O. Box 91
Mission, Kansas 66201

Dedication

For Narelle Todd, whose creativity, vision, and caring have led me to a better writing career—and a better life.

Don't miss out on any of the magic.
Subscribe to Cassandra Chandler's newsletter at
cassandra-chandler.com!

Chapter One

Five weeks, two days, eleven hours, and thirty-five minutes. That was how long Lord Snow had been in the mortal realm training the new Lord and Lady of the North Wind for their duties. He was ready to go home.

While the mortal realm wasn't quite the pit that most of the Fae thought, Snow still didn't want to hang around any longer than he had to. They called him 'the Krampus,' by the Gods' sake, and made up horrible stories about him. *Him*—the Lord of Endless Snow. Why would he want to stick around a place like that?

Across the main room of the Yuletide Bakery, his best friend, North snuck up behind his mate, Melanie, and wrapped his arms around her waist to pull her against his chest in a hug. She laughed and swatted at him, trying to arrange a plate of cookies in their bakery. Snow's newest friends, Aidan and Sylvia—also known as the White Stag and... the Fae Lady soon to be known as the White Doe—observed, also laughing. Aidan darted forward and snatched a handful of the cookies, earning him a playful swat of his own from Melanie and a look of reproach.

Snow's heart ached oddly and he rubbed the spot. It felt hollow, like something was missing in his chest. The mortal realm often had this effect on him. He didn't like it. The longer they stayed, the stronger the feeling became. He was certain it would also make it harder for Aidan and Sylvia to leave.

"It's time," Snow said, his voice calm and low, yet carrying across the space.

The others froze in place, their smiles falling. Aidan and Sylvia looked to each other and nodded, but Melanie rushed forward.

"It's too soon," she said. "They need more training."

Snow shook his head. "They're more than ready. The longer we wait, the more angry the Winter Queen will become at our absence."

"All the more reason to—"

"Melanie," Sylvia said. "It's okay. Really, it's okay." She looked to Snow with a smile that suffused the hollowness in his chest. At least it also warmed the space. "If Snow says we're ready, we're ready."

North pulled Aidan into a bro hug and clapped the man on the back. "Remember everything I taught you. You'll be a fine Lord of the North Wind."

"I learned from the best," Aidan said.

Melanie's eyes filled with tears, but she forced herself to smile as she hugged Sylvia as well. "You'll come to visit me, right?"

"As often as I can." Sylvia kissed Melanie's dark hair before pulling back.

All of them had become so close during Aidan and Sylvia's training. Snow hated to separate them from their friends, but it was inevitable. If things went well, they would be able to come and go from the mortal realm whenever they liked. If things didn't go well…

This will work. It has to work.

Snow had several contingency plans, each more desperate than the last. He was certain he wouldn't have to use any of them. He stood straighter, exuding confidence to help inspire those who looked up to him. Aidan caught his eye and nodded, then offered his arm to Sylvia. The pair approached Snow with perfect posture, shoulders back and heads held high like the Fairy Lord and Lady that they had become. Snow smiled down at them, then pulled them into a hug. He was so proud of all they had learned.

The Winter Queen would accept them. He was sure of it.

The castle seemed bigger than Snow remembered. And much, much colder. Spending weeks in the mortal realm had made him too accustomed to warmth. He led Aidan and Sylvia toward the throne room, pausing briefly to glance at their attire and make sure the magical clothes he had fashioned for them were acceptable.

Sylvia's red hair was a flame against the white gown she wore. The fabric sparkled with diamonds that gleamed in the light cast from the crystal walls of the castle. A mesh of diamonds in platinum chains held her hair in a chignon and a white silk cape lined with gray-specked fur was fastened around her shoulders.

Aidan wore a similar cape, along with a princely jacket that suited his new station. Or at least the station that Snow was hoping he would soon officially be bestowed. His dark hair was a sharp contrast to the white clothing Snow had created for him.

"You're going to do great," Snow said quietly as they entered the room. "Just remember everything I taught you."

The Winter Queen sat on her crystal throne in the middle of an enormous dais. The entire room had been grown from magical crystal that glowed from within, granting a soft light to the space. Usually, two ornate thrones sat at her sides, one for Lord Snow and the other for Lord North. Today, there were none. Snow led Aidan and Sylvia to the center of the room, then approached the Queen's throne and bowed deeply.

After a silence that stretched on for several minutes, the Winter Queen said, "Lord Snow, you have been gone far longer than expected. I had begun to wonder if you, too, had abandoned me."

"Never, my Queen," Snow said, rising to meet her stern gaze. "I regret that it took me too long to succumb to your wisdom. I see now that North is lost to us."

His stomach churned with nerves. Did she know that North was still the Yule Cat? And that Snow had defied her decrees in so many other ways? He was certain that she would be happy with his choices eventually, but not so sure she could forgive his willingness to go against what she had proclaimed.

"I have done as you said and brought back the Lord of the North Wind." He swallowed hard, hoping fervently that she would accept Aidan and Sylvia. If the Queen rejected them, he would protect them. Any punishment would fall on his shoulders alone. He'd make sure of it.

"Yet I do not see Jack Frost," she said, looking pointedly over the heads of Aidan and Sylvia.

"True, but I bring another." He gestured toward Aidan. "I present to you the new Lord and Lady of the North Wind."

Aidan bowed low and Sylvia curtseyed, both of them holding the postures of deference, their eyes cast down to the floor.

"You present to me the new Lord and Lady of the North Wind?" the Winter Queen said. "Their manners are better than the last 'new Lady' you brought before me, but that hardly makes up for defying me. I know that North remains the Yule Cat. And now you have taken the power I entrusted to you and placed it within these people who are unknown to me."

"Majesty, I beg your forgiveness," Snow said, bowing even lower than before. "I could not bring myself to take away the essence that North was born with. He has been the Yule Cat for as long as I have been... the Krampus." He hated claiming the name, but knew the importance of this moment. "When you found us, you saw potential and gifted us with powers to serve you better, to serve the Yuletide Kingdom. I believe that North can yet be of service to us, but this pair will be an even better Lord and Lady of the North Wind."

"And why would you think that?" she asked in an imperious voice.

Snow stood, then nodded to Aidan and Sylvia, stepping away. Aidan took Sylvia's hand and nodded to her as well, no doubt encouraging her. She was trembling slightly from nerves. The cold no longer affected her after gaining the powers Snow had granted to her—some of which she was more proficient at than others. Shifting... she was still getting used to.

Silver light covered their bodies, suffusing their forms until they were merely silhouettes. Their shapes began changing, antlers sprouting from their heads, faces becoming muzzles, and bodies falling forward onto four legs as they assumed their deer forms. The light withdrew, leaving them white as snow, their coats gleaming with inner radiance. Their antlers were gold and put off their own light, as did their golden irises.

The Winter Queen's eyes widened as she rose from her throne, her hands clasped tightly in front of her. She took a step forward, then another and another. When she reached the steps, she hurried down them, approaching the White Stag and the White Doe with what Snow hoped was wonder in her eyes. She reached out to touch them, and Snow held his breath. Though Aidan and Sylvia were skittish in this form, neither flinched as the Winter Queen rested her hands on their muzzles.

"Oh, Krampus," the Queen said, a wistful note in her voice that he had never heard before. "You have done well."

She continued to touch both Sylvia and Aidan's faces, even going so far as to stroke their foreheads lightly. Snow couldn't believe the wonder in her expressive face as she looked at them. His heart gave a little tug as he realized he had never seen her truly happy. Not as he'd seen North and Melanie being, nor Aidan and Sylvia. For the briefest moment, Snow wondered what that would feel like for himself. He quickly buried the thought.

"You will be wondrous additions to my court," the Queen said, resting one of her hands on each of the deer's cheeks.

Her expression clouded, her eyebrows pinching together and her smile fading as she stepped back, pulling her hands away as if startled. Aidan followed, as did Sylvia. Krampus was about to intervene, uncertain of what was going on, but all they did was gently bump their noses against her arms. The Queen's lips tightened and she pulled her fisted hands up to her heart, holding them there like a shield.

Aidan dropped to his knees in a cumbersome bow for his current stag form. He bowed his head so low that his nose touched the ground. Sylvia looked over at him, then made a disgruntled squeak. Her legs shook as she gingerly maneuvered herself into a position they had never practiced in this form.

Sylvia stared at the knees of her forelegs—which did not bend at all the way her elbows did when those limbs were arms—then let out a sigh and started to lower herself. Snow held his breath to see if she could manage it. At first, it looked as though she would make it, but then she started to lose her balance. Aidan began to rise, but it was the Queen who reached Sylvia first.

The tall woman launched herself forward, wrapping her arms around Sylvia's chest and steadying her. Together, the women lowered themselves to the ground. Sylvia's ears flicked with interest as she looked up into the Queen's wide green eyes. The doe bowed her head in the Queen's embrace.

"You may be in the form that is of greatest ease to you, child," the Queen said.

Silver light swept over Sylvia as she reverted to her human form. She was still on all fours on the floor. Snow wanted to cover his eyes and shake his head, but he also couldn't look away from the scene unfolding before him. The Queen kept her hold on Sylvia, grasping her elbows and helping her rise amid the voluminous folds of her gown.

The Queen glanced at Snow as they rose, her cheeks actually flushing pink for the first time—in his presence at least. This was so much better than he had even hoped. The Queen was not only accepting Aidan and Sylvia, but seemed delighted by them. He was well on his way to bringing his family back together again. He just had to get the Queen to forgive North for choosing Melanie over his duty to her.

The Queen turned to Aidan and said, "You as well, Lord North."

Snow's cheeks pinched as he felt the biggest smile he'd ever had stretch his face. She had accepted Aidan. Snow was sure she would accept Sylvia, too. Aidan glowed bright silver as he rose up on his back legs, resuming his human form. He bowed again, and the Queen angled her head toward him in response.

She pulled Sylvia up the steps of the dais with her. As they approached the throne, two more chairs grew from the crystal floor—smaller, of course, but just as ornate and beautiful. Snow felt his mouth drop open as the Queen swirled her finger and a cushion appeared on the chair at her left. She set Sylvia on it, then turned to Aidan and gestured him toward the other seat. With a quick glance to Snow, Aidan hurried after them. He didn't sit until the Queen did.

Snow's heart was pounding in his throat. She had definitely accepted them, but there was a coldness in her bearing as she looked at him. His misgiving grew when she turned to him with a distinct frown.

"You have done well in bringing me Lord North and Lady... Silver," the Queen said. "But that does not excuse your defiance. I had expected Jack Frost to be among my court."

Snow opened his mouth to say something, but snapped it shut. Sylvia was squirming in her seat, obviously also wanting to jump in, but they had gone over this time and time again. The Queen had a temper that burned icy hot. It was best not to get in the way of it.

He dropped to one knee, bowing his head deeply. "Majesty, I beg your forgiveness," he said.

Silence grew in the room. Snow's heart was a constant drumbeat in his ears. If she exiled him, as she had North, then Aidan and Sylvia would be on their own navigating their new duties. He didn't want that for them. Snow knew that his subjects could keep things running. He had trained them well. But this was his home. He had done all of this because the Queen and her court and all their subjects were his family. He didn't want to lose that.

"Forgiveness is something that takes time," she said, her voice barely above a whisper. "And sometimes distance as well."

Was she banishing him? He wasn't sure. Her demeanor was so unlike what he was used to. Again, the silence stretched on.

"Lord Snow," she said.

He closed his eyes and let out a huge breath, the tension knotting his back easing somewhat. She still called him 'Lord Snow.' He wasn't being banished.

"Return to the mortal realm," she said. "I will summon you to return when I am ready."

When would that be? How long did she need him to stay away? She hadn't said he couldn't contact anyone in the Yuletide Kingdom, so he would be able to check in with his seneschals, but still… His mind filled with a thousand questions, scenarios, and endless lists of tasks required to keep things running well. It had only been himself alone for so long while North was in exile—an exile Snow had hoped to ease, not share.

"Majesty, if I may?" Sylvia said in a gentle voice.

Snow's heart sank. He didn't want her to get in the middle of this. Things were going too well for them. He didn't dare look up, but he heard the swish of fabric as Sylvia approached him. She wrapped her arms around his shoulders, her hug bringing her lips close to his ear.

"We'll be okay, you can trust us," she whispered. "Just give her the time she needs." Sylvia rose and returned to her spot at the Queen's side.

"You are kind," the Queen said. "As can I be as well."

"Of course, majesty," Snow said.

He stood, but didn't dare look up at her. He did give Aidan a quick nod. The White Stag's eyes were wide, his jaw tense. Why wouldn't he be nervous, watching his ally and mentor leave him in a situation where Snow was supposed to be to guide him through?

His heart was heavy as he walked from the throne room. Once more, he had disappointed his Queen. Worse, Aidan and Sylvia were being left to navigate this tricky situation on their own. Snow had at least prepared his seneschals for such an eventuality, but he had thought it an unlikely scenario for the new Lord and Lady.

His steps were slow as he ascended the steps that would lead him outside of the castle. This wasn't the start Aidan and Sylvia deserved. Most of all, he hated the feeling that he had failed them.

Chapter Two

The Yuletide Bakery always had something special going on. Christmas was the biggest holiday of the year, of course, with the bakery being Christmas-themed year round, but the owner, North Cotter, dressed up the store for every holiday Spring had heard of and several that she hadn't. He baked special holiday-themed cookies as well as serving everyone's perennial favorites. Valentine's Day was no exception.

Bright red hearts that seemed to sparkle from within dangled from the ceiling or hung against the weathered brick walls. The ever-present tree glittered with silver, gold, and red ornaments that continued the theme. Little silver sculptures of lovers kissing or embracing— tastefully, of course—sat along the tops of the display cases. Inside the cases, all kinds of chocolate treats, cookies, and petit fours delighted the eye before delighting the tastebuds. This was truly one of her happiest places.

Spring was sitting at one of the tall tables near the main display cases and the register in a sort of nook nestled between the tree and a rough-hewn stone fireplace that crackled with a lovely fire. The nook was partially under a staircase that wrapped around two walls heading for the second story. It wasn't her favorite place to sit, but it was warm and cozy, and she could see and hear all the most interesting happenings while staying out of everyone's way.

The bakery was hopping. People came in to buy boxes of heart-shaped cookies for Valentine's Day office parties or more specialized pastries as gifts or self-indulgences. The baristas were doing brisk business as well, what with all the snow piling on. Ever since Christmas, it seemed like there was a steady stream of flakes coming down. Spring loved the wintery weather and all the cozy sweaters, stylish coats, and cute matching hats, gloves, and scarves involved, but she was starting to really look forward to… well, spring.

Everything in its own time.

She didn't want to rush through one of her favorite holidays, even if she was spending this one on her own. She settled into her spot as she took a sip of her frappé coffee. The sweetened condensed milk was perfectly balanced with the bitter coffee. Knowing she'd be tucked away near the fire, she had opted for the cold beverage to help keep her from overheating in the snug space.

She had brought her own travel mug, and sipped from the built-in straw as she looked out over the bakery. Several tables had families sitting around them. Her smile softened as she watched a mother with a toddler sitting on her knee, her arms tight around the child's middle as she gave him a hug. He lifted a heart-shaped sugar cookie to feed it to her and they both laughed as it took him several tries to get his aim right for her mouth.

A familiar pain lanced through Spring's chest along with the warmth of the moment. Not physical pain—but the pain of loss. She would never have children of her own. Fate had other plans for her. At least, that's what Spring chose to believe when doctor after doctor told her the same thing. Maybe she couldn't have her own family, but she could use her PR company to help support non-profits that supported families in need. Her team did regular pro-bono work with several local foster care and adoption agencies, and she donated a hefty amount of their profits to social services organizations that helped children.

She put her hand over her heart and took a deep breath in through her nose, then blew it out slowly through her mouth, visualizing a golden light soothing the hurt and filling her heart with warmth. Someday, she'd meet a man who understood her circumstances and how she felt about it and would support her in her own dreams of fostering.

Luck hadn't been on her side with that so far, either. The few guys she'd been serious with who had said they were okay with her goals and her situation eventually bailed. That was fine with her, though. No serious relationships meant more time to build up her company and devote to her charity work. Plus, it gave her more opportunities to enjoy herself with the men who caught her eye.

As if summoned by her thought, a huge man strode past her table, circling around behind the out-of-the-way display case that was nearest the staircase Spring was tucked beneath. He must be pushing seven feet tall and looked like he spent most of his day at the gym bulking up. His gait was filled with confidence, his bearing clearly broadcasting that he was the absolute alpha in the room. Of course, he hadn't met Spring yet. She smirked at the idea of how that introduction might go, tingling warmth spreading over her arms and back as she imagined different scenarios.

He walked right to North, who was working behind the display case, and the two men stood chatting quietly. With his chiseled jaw, and constantly windswept hair, North was as easy on the eyes as his baked goods were on the tongue. Spring was sure many of the female clientele for the bakery came in just to see him, though they were in for a disappointment. He had acquired a shadow recently in the form of a lovely brunette with big blue eyes, pale skin, and a smile that made it impossible to hate her, even if she'd landed one of the most eligible bachelors in town.

North was nice to look at, but Spring had never pined for him. He was too much like the guys she usually dated, and honestly, she was so bored with 'the usual.' Maybe that was why her heart seemed to stutter when the new man flexed his back, his muscles rippling beneath his dark blue three-piece suit. It probably cost as much as a small car. The silky material of his jacket accentuated his broad shoulders and hugged his massive biceps. His slacks showcased his long legs and muscular thighs.

Yeah, Spring was pretty smitten. It had been a long time since she'd been so attracted to a man. Actually, the more she thought about it, she'd never been this attracted to someone before. She took another sip of her frappé, watching the pair as they stood near enough for her to hear every word of their conversation. Although, the more she listened, the less it made sense.

"Look, it's been less than a week," the huge man said.

"I know." North shook his head." All I'm saying is that I think you should be asking Malachi to step in for them more. Help them out with the political stuff."

"And have them be seen as weak by the other courts when they're making their first impressions?" the man said. "No way."

North shook his head. "It won't be seen as weakness, Snow."

Snow? That huge, gorgeous, incredibly well-dressed guy was named *Snow*?

"Just because Melanie blew it—" Snow said.

"Hey!" The brunette was actually with them, though

she was so small, Spring hadn't been able to see her at first, the men blocking her from view. Now, Spring had a name for her, too.

"Come on, man," North said, pulling Melanie against his side as she glared at Snow.

Snow took a deep breath, expanding his chest to an incredible size, then let it out slowly. The silken fabric of his jacket pulled across the muscles of his back, the seams straining to hold together. Spring could relate. She pulled her lower lip between her teeth, imagining what it would be like to slide her hands along those shoulders. Maybe while he grasped her hips and they slow-danced to some soft jazz music.

"Okay." Snow's rumbly voice grew tighter as he spoke. "Just because Melanie didn't know what she was doing and made an epically bad first impression..." He trailed off, noticing how North and Melanie stared at him.

North shrugged to Melanie. "That's probably as good an apology as we're going to get."

Melanie frowned, but she was the one to speak next. "We were just thinking that if Malachi was able to give them a little more guidance, maybe they could work together and find a way to help spring return."

Snow shook his head. "Everyone keeps forgetting that I'm the Lord of Endless Snow. *Snow*. Not spring. You know what spring has going for it?"

North and Melanie looked at each other and shrugged.

"Not snow, that's what," Snow said.

Spring busted out with a laugh. She couldn't help it. Snow glanced over his shoulder at her, his lips a thin, disapproving line. Oh goodness, he was even better to look at from the front. Black hair close-cropped against his scalp, though a bit longer on the top, strong features, dark eyes that seemed to bore into her. Her skin rose in goosebumps as he quickly assessed her, then glanced back again, as if the first look hadn't been quite enough. She smirked at him, lifting her phone and intimating that she had been scrolling through messages when she laughed. He was so huge, it was easy to see him in her periphery when he turned his attention back to his friends.

"I have to go help out in the kitchen," Melanie said. "But give it some thought."

She squeezed Snow's arm, then stood on her tip toes and stared at him expectantly. He sighed and shifted his weight from one foot to the other, then bent down so that she could plant a quick kiss on his cheek. North didn't seem the least bit jealous, so Spring didn't see why she should be. Besides, she couldn't keep from smiling at the sweet gesture, or the way Snow's posture had relaxed a little when he straightened. Both men watched Melanie hurry through the kitchen door.

"I know you mean well and you want the best for us all," North said. "But ignoring this won't help anyone. It's time. We need to make a move to try to—"

"Try to what?" Snow said. "Start a rebellion?"

"Hell no." North actually took a step back, shaking his head emphatically. "Try to help the Winter Queen," he said. "Bringing back spring will mean she's healed. It'll mean the whole kingdom is healed."

Kingdom? Winter Queen? This was starting to sound like a fairy tale. Maybe they were in a play together. Except, the seriousness on both men's faces struck her as absolutely real.

"I need to help out the others in the kitchen," North said. He also reached out and gripped Snow's arm, then leaned in as if to plant one on him. Snow recoiled and flailed his arms, making North retreat.

"What, no sugar for me?" North said, feigning confusion.

"Get out of here," Snow said, an exasperated note to his voice.

North kept laughing all the way through the kitchen door while Snow stood with his hands on his hips, shaking his head. The view was spectacular, but Spring was done being a spectator. She slid from her stool and approached him from behind so he wouldn't see her till she was ready.

"Everybody's so in love with spring," Snow murmured. "I don't get it. It's just a season. Has a lot of flowers. So what?"

"Wow, were you born that cynical, or has life just been too hard on you?"

Spring made sure that she was standing in the perfect pose to catch his attention when he turned. Arms crossed over her chest to plump her breasts, one hip stuck out at a cocky, yet alluring angle. She plastered her best 'I know a secret you don't know' smirk on her face and waited to assess his reaction. This one wouldn't be an easy conquest.

"Excuse me?" he said, looming over her.

The shirt beneath his jacket and vest was such a dark blue, it was nearly black. His midnight blue tie caught the light and sparkled almost like there were diamonds or stars woven into the fabric.

"Do you think you intimidate me just because you're huge?" She shook her head, stepping closer. "The bigger they are, the harder they fall." Her smirk deepened as she leaned close, daring to run a fingertip over the lapel of his suit. "Besides, I'm a size queen."

"What does that even…" He shook his head, but she noticed him intently studying her again. He didn't seem to know what to make of her. Finally he took in a deep breath and said, "It's bad manners to listen in on other people's conversations."

Running to the rules for a rescue? She could work with that. She lifted his tie, delighting in the silken texture and mesmerized by the starlike pattern that seemed to dance and weave among the fibers. Looking up at him, she gave it a bit of a tug, then let the fabric slip through her fingers.

"Well, if you think I've been naughty, you're welcome

to spank me," she said.

His eyebrows shot up and his mouth dropped open. It wasn't quite the reaction she had expected or hoped for, but it was definitely entertaining. The way she figured it, either he would take her up on her offer, and they would have a grand time together, or he'd be intrigued enough to ask her out maybe.

Of course, there was the chance he'd be offended and storm off. That would be a helpful reaction, too. If he couldn't laugh at himself or let loose and have a little fun, there was no way she would want to start something with him. Deep down, she had a feeling he was a softy, though. And the idea of unraveling that tightly wound exterior was an irresistible challenge.

"But you're the one being rude and badmouthing spring," she said.

"What the hell do you care what I think of it?" he said.

"Well, for one, it's a glorious season, full of hope and promise."

He crossed his arms over his truly massive chest. "And allergens."

"And bunnies."

"Aha," he said, pointing a finger at her as he towered over her. "Winter has bunnies, too."

"But those are cold bunnies." She stepped closer, and pushed her mouth into just enough of a pout to draw his attention to her lips. "Don't you want the bunnies to be warm?"

"I don't…" He blinked a few times, his voice trailing off as he stared at her mouth. "Wait, what?"

He was even cuter when he was flustered. His glance actually dropped to her cleavage briefly, his eyebrows pulling more tightly together over his eyes.

Oh, this guy would be really fun. That much passion crammed into such an amazing package. She wanted to be the one to loosen the hinges and watch it fly everywhere.

"I don't care if spring ever comes." He said each word forcefully, again stepping closer. The lapels of his very expensive suit brushed against her chest.

She bit the inside of her cheek to keep from laughing. In a low voice that had him leaning closer to hear her, she said, "Then you are never taking me to dinner."

"Why would I want to?" he said, his voice exasperated.

She arched an eyebrow at him and cocked her head to the side, pouting her lips. A muscle in his jaw started to twitch as she let the silence stretch on.

"And why can't I?" he finally demanded.

She ran her fingertips under the lapels of his suit, smoothing them, then brushed her hand down along his tie with just enough pressure to tantalize him.

"Well, that's the other reason I care what you think of this particular season," she said. She lifted his tie, then used it to pull him closer as she rose on her tip-toes. With her lips a breath away from his ear, she whispered,

"Because my name is Spring."

Chapter Three

What was wrong with this mortal? The things she said didn't make any sense, but the way she talked drew Snow in. Her hair was gold as warm sunlight, spilling over her shoulders in soft waves. Her large blue eyes sparkled with mirth even when she wasn't laughing, and her smirk made him feel like he was missing out on something important. Something he needed to know. Worst of all, she wouldn't stop touching him.

She said her name was Spring, and a thrum of magic let him know she spoke the truth. For a moment, he wondered if perhaps she was from the Court of the Springtime Fae, but none of them would carry that name. He doubted the embodiment of spring itself would have manifested just to drop by and talk to him, even with all the happenings in the Yuletide Kingdom.

No, this was a mortal. A strange, compelling, aggravating mortal.

"This is when you tell me your name," Spring said. "It's only polite."

"Names carry power. They aren't to be tossed around

lightly."

"I can't just call you Snow."

"Aha, I knew you were listening."

Her lips pulled into an odd frown, almost like an upside-down smirk. "What I heard didn't make any sense. And it doesn't really count as eavesdropping when people are standing right next to you having a conversation as if you aren't there."

"We didn't know you were there."

"Did you expect me to get up and leave?" she asked, dropping his tie and placing one fisted hand on her hip. "Flail my arms and say, 'Guys, I can hear you' maybe?"

"I expected you not to come up and talk to me like… Like…"

"Like what?"

She stepped closer, whispers of her perfume swirling around him with the light scent of flowers. The sweet fragrance clouded his mind. Everything about this woman was clouding his mind, and he didn't have time for it. When she reached for his tie again, he stood straighter and pulled the fabric from her fingers, tucking it back beneath his vest and smoothing it down.

"Like you know me," Snow said. "You don't." The words sent an odd pang through him, fluttering within that hollowness in his chest.

"True," she said. "But I'd like to."

Something in him sparked, a quick bolt of energy

charging along his nerves and sending tingles of awareness over his flesh. The way she looked at him, the warmth in her eyes and smile... It was dangerous. Mostly because he wanted more. He wanted to explore what that sultry smile meant and unravel the secrets hidden in that mysterious smirk.

The smirk was the worst. And the single arched eyebrow. She was staring at him as if she knew secrets that not even he was privy to. He didn't like it.

"Why do you always have that smile on your face?" he said.

Her eyebrows both lifted at that. "Wow, that's a refreshing change. Usually guys are always telling women to smile, but you prefer a scowl." She cocked her head to the side, her smirk softening a bit. "Spoiler alert. I'm going to smile if I want to. But maybe I'll throw you a scowl from time to time. If you earn it."

"Lucky me."

She brought her beverage up to her mouth while holding his focus, lips slowly parting before wrapping around the straw. Somehow, the sight sent more of those electric tingles zinging through his body. His hands opened and curled into fists, and he had the strangest urge to grab her and pull her closer.

"What is that thing that you're drinking?" he asked, scowling.

"This?" Spring took another sip of her drink, holding

their eye contact and smirking as she did. "It's a frappé. Want some?"

She held the drink out to him, but he shook his head.

"What the heck is a frappé?"

"Coffee and condensed milk over ice." She lifted the cup and stared at it, assessing. "It's cold and bitter at first, but really sweet once you get used to it."

As she said the last, she lowered her drink and winked at him. He found himself leaning forward, his body inching closer to her. She was a distraction, and he did not have time to be distracted. Too many people were counting on him. He pulled himself back, shaking his head.

"You seem really…" His voice trailed off. What did she seem like?

Provocative. Beautiful. Aggressive.

"*Aggressive*," he said, a bit louder than he intended.

That's what it was that intrigued him. Well, among a host of other things. Another wave of appreciative heat flowed through him. He respected when people went after what they wanted with everything they had. But he didn't know what she wanted or who she was or what her hidden motives were. Everyone had hidden motives and agendas. With the Yuletide Kingdom going through so many transitions, he didn't dare let himself slip.

"I know what I want and I'm not afraid to go after it." She lowered her voice as she went on so that once more he had to bend closer to hear her. "And between you and me,

I usually get it."

He straightened again, shaking his head. She was too good at drawing him in. He stepped away, straightening his tie.

"If you'll excuse me," he said. "I have business to attend to."

"I bet you do."

That damn smirk of hers. What did she know that he didn't? What was she hiding?

He didn't have time to unravel her mysteries. She was mortal. That was all he needed to know about her. Mortals had no business with the Fae. He turned and walked away, hurrying through the bakery toward the front door. He swore he could feel her eyes on him the entire time.

As soon as he was outside, he took a deep breath of the freezing winter air. It flooded his lungs, invigorating him. This was his season, his energy, his power. This, he understood. He was the Lord of Endless Snow. And he did have business he needed to tend to.

He turned toward his closest office, his long strides carrying him quickly over the sidewalk. Three steps from the bakery's front door, his foot hit a patch of glassy ice and flew out from under him. He flipped up into the air and landed flat on his back, the wind knocked out of him.

That should not have happened. He should have sensed the ice on the ground, just as he could feel the energy of the snow all around him. This was his season, except…

Except he shared it with others. Others who held sway over the elements of cold, just as he controlled the snow.

"Frost," he rumbled, banging his head against the sidewalk beneath him.

Jack Frost had warned Snow that Frost would be tormenting him. This was just the sort of trickery for which the other Fae was famous. Actually, it would probably get much worse. Snow didn't have time for this. He needed to find Frost and confront him. Wring his little neck until he understood that the Lord of Endless Snow was not to be messed with.

As he was about to rise, a hint of clear sky broke through the thick clouds above, the robin's egg blue a striking contrast. Snow held still, seeking out the energy that had managed to break through the cloud cover he'd been generating for days. He closed his eyes for a moment, centering himself, but whatever had caused the break in the clouds was gone. When he opened his eyes, Spring was standing above him, her eyebrows drawn together in concern.

"Are you okay?" she asked. "I saw you fall through the bakery's window."

"I'm fine," Snow grumbled.

She arched an eyebrow and gestured toward him with her beverage. "Then why are you still lying on the ground?"

He sighed. "I'm contemplating the life choices that

have led me to this moment."

At least he understood the tiny smirk that brought to her mouth. What he didn't understand was the odd flutter in his chest that stirred in response to it.

"I bet you could use a little Spring pick-me-up now," she said, offering her free hand.

He waved it away, rolling to his side and leaping to his feet. "I don't need spring," he bit out each word.

"Wow, you are a cranky bear," she said, scowling.

"What?" Snow said, nearly gasping.

Movement across the street caught his eye. Leaning against one of the buildings, a tall, lanky man watched them with piercing ice-blue eyes. His dark hair stood out in an unkempt mess and equally dark eyebrows lowered as he cast a smirk that was much less pleasant toward them.

"Frost," Snow growled. He was going to put a stop to this once and for all.

Snow stalked forward, but someone grabbed the back of his jacket. He spun around to face the new threat, but he slipped on the icy ground again. He was vaguely aware of someone grabbing his jacket, but kept spinning, arms flailing as he fell to the ground. This time, a light weight landed on top of him. Seconds later, a bus careened past. It hit a pothole near the curb, filled with thick, cold slush that erupted from under its tire, dousing Snow. He looked down to see Spring lying across his chest, her hair a wet mess and eyes wide.

"What the…" Snow quickly rose, pulling her up with him. He turned back to the alley, but Frost was gone. Snow had missed his chance. Growling, he turned to Spring and bellowed, "What did you do that for?"

"Excuse me? I was trying to stop you from being hit by a bus," she yelled back.

"What do I care about a bus?"

Her eyes widened and her mouth opened and closed a few times in the first response he clearly understood from her. Exasperation.

"Who doesn't care about being hit by a bus?" Her voice rose as she spoke, ending as a high squeak.

Before Snow could respond, Melanie ran out from the bakery.

"Oh my gosh, are you guys okay?" She wrapped her arm around Spring's waist and immediately continued. "What am I saying? Of course you're not okay. You're freezing. Come inside. You'll turn into an icicle if you try to walk home like this."

"Thank you," Spring said, still scowling at Snow.

Something about the change in her demeanor made that aching hollowness flare up in Snow's chest again. There was no playful scowl, no teasing glances. The warmth had changed to an icy cold, and for once, he didn't like it.

"North and I live above the bakery," Melanie said. "You can get dried off and warmed up."

"That sounds nice and very considerate," Spring said,

angling her head to glare at Snow. "Kind of like stopping someone from being hit by a bus."

"I would have been fine," Snow snapped.

Spring let out a little disgusted grunt and shook her head. "I was wrong about you," she said. She turned away, letting Melanie lead her into the bakery.

"Wrong how?" Snow called after them.

The door swung shut.

He stood in the slush for a few moments, replaying the last few moments and trying to figure out exactly when everything had careened completely out of control. Out of *his* control, anyway. Frost was probably having the time of his life. But Spring had gotten caught up in their issues, and that was unacceptable. She had stopped Snow from confronting Frost and...

And she had pulled Snow back when he'd been about to step in front of a bus. Sure, he could have summoned a bank of snow to sweep him away from danger with only a thought. The driver might have had a scare, but would have felt better when the wipers cleared the windshield and all they saw was snow.

Spring didn't know about Snow's powers. She had seen what she thought was a mortal man on the verge of ending his mortal existence in a potentially very painful way. Not to mention the emotional turmoil it would have caused to the driver and passengers. The turmoil it would have caused her to witness.

In her mind, she had saved him, and he was sure it had been instinct. As she'd said, she knew what she wanted, and she went for it. She wanted him to be safe. She wanted to get to know him. At least, she *had* wanted to. Now, she thought she was wrong about him. But what did that even mean?

Her words rang through his mind, echoing in that hollow place in his chest. The clouds began to drop thick flakes of snow, coating his shoulders and sticking to the slush that had soaked through his jacket. His skin prickled, his scalp itched where his horns had once been. He clenched his hands into fists and yelled, "Wrong how?"

His control was slipping. His muscles bunched with the urge to change—to his new form. The form the Winter Queen had given him. But beneath it, he felt the old. He felt the Krampus lying in wait. Always waiting for him to make a mistake. To lose everything that he'd been given. Everything that he'd worked for and held dear.

This mortal woman was a threat to his existence. A threat to his new nature, possibly his sanity. And yet, he couldn't turn away from the building. Instead, he stalked to the door and tore it open, the hinges creaking in protest and the bell above the door jangling in distress. Snow ignored the stares of the people inside and headed straight up the staircase to North and Melanie's apartment above. Headed straight for Spring.

Chapter Four

"Are you all right? What happened?" North met Melanie and Spring at the door of the bakery, his eyes wide as he looked Spring over. She cringed to think of what a mess she must be.

Her coat was soaked and her hair was a filthy mess. She could see gray clods of slush stuck to their ends. She was going to need a deep conditioning treatment after this. But instead of complaining, she forced herself to smile, pulling her best professional persona to the surface and stuffing the seething anger deep beneath.

"I'm fine," she said, but even she could hear the strain in her voice.

"We're going to go upstairs so she can clean up," Melanie said. "Can you handle the cookies for a while till I get back?"

"Forget the cookies." North glanced out the front windows, grimacing. His usually-smiling lips were pulled in a deep frown and his eyebrows lowered ominously. "How could Snow let this happen to you?"

"Leave it," Spring said.

She'd seen enough fights to know when one was brewing—and that North didn't stand a chance against Snow. Even after everything, the thought sent a little thrill shooting up and down her spine. If something had happened between herself and Snow, she definitely would have felt safe staying out late with him. Though, it would have been more fun to stay in…

"You sure you're okay?" North said, turning his attention fully back to her.

Spring's smile was a bit more sincere as she looked over to Melanie and said, "We girls have got this, right?"

Melanie's eyes widened, and she smiled back, nodding eagerly. "Yeah, we do."

"Don't let those amazing cookies burn." Spring nodded toward the kitchen.

"If you're sure." North slowly backed away, watching them as if he expected them to change their minds.

"Come on," Spring said, heading up the staircase as Melanie eagerly followed.

A door on the second level right above the kitchen led into one of the most gorgeous apartments Spring had ever seen. Melanie paused to pull off her shoes in the entryway, and Spring followed her example, taking the opportunity to study the intricate tile flooring just past the door. Each tile was a mosaic of blues and whites, with a swirling pattern that reminded her of a windy day.

"The bathroom is just in here," Melanie said, leading

her through a living room with plush carpets that Spring's feet sank into.

Soft, romantic jazz filtered through the air from speakers Spring couldn't see, and a fire sprang up in the fireplace as they crossed the room, the fake logs glowing cheerily in seconds. Spring was tempted to just plop herself down on the gray faux fur rug in front of it, but she shuddered at the thought of what the mess in her hair would turn into if it dried in place. A couple of chairs and a matching large, poofy couch sat a ways back from the fireplace, a soft fleece blanket draped over its back that was equally tempting.

Spring hadn't worn her warmest clothes for this outing. She had on a dark red woolen skirt that ended just below her knees with a brighter red button-up sweater—her favorite Valentine's Day outfit for when she was going out-and-about as opposed to how she dressed up for a fancy evening with a date. Thankfully, she'd opted for dark tights. White would have stained terribly. The black boots she'd left at the door had protected her from the brunt of the slush that hit her legs. Her favorite red peacoat had taken most of the damage. She had no idea how she would ever get it clean again.

Melanie led her into a cozy bathroom with a tub and a shower. Spring wasn't looking forward to trying to stick her head under that to rinse her hair, but she was not comfortable with the idea of taking a shower at a stranger's house. At least the shower head was detachable.

"There are plenty of towels in here," Melanie said, pointing to a cabinet in the wall. "This is the guest bathroom, so everything hanging out is fresh and clean. Please feel free to use anything you want. I don't think my clothes will fit you, but I can bring you some of North's while we wash your outfit. I'll leave them outside the door here."

"I think most of it just got on my coat," Spring said.

"Yeah." Melanie pulled a face. "It's such a beautiful coat. I think I can get most of that out, though."

"It's okay, I don't want to trouble you."

Melanie smiled, her blue eyes sparkling. "It's no trouble at all. Snow is family and I appreciate what you did for him."

"At least someone did," Spring mumbled under her breath.

"He really is a nice guy underneath." Melanie half-shrugged. "He just hasn't quite figured out how to show it."

Spring snorted. "Trust me, I know the type and have had my fill of it."

Melanie's smile faded and it was almost as if the lights dimmed in the room. She was such a sweet person.

"Hey, I'm sorry," Spring said. "I'm just grumpy because I'm covered in slush."

"Then let me help you with that."

She was so earnest. Spring didn't want to disappoint her. She nodded, then carefully slid her coat down her arms, trying not to let anything splat on the floor as she did. Most of the slush had already fallen off—probably in the entryway to the bakery or on the stairs.

"I'm so sorry, I must have made such a mess when I came back inside the bakery."

"Don't worry about it." Melanie was already scrutinizing the coat. She beamed up at Spring and said, "I'll make Snow clean it up."

Both women laughed, then Melanie headed for the door.

"If you need anything, just call me," Melanie said. "But maybe be a little loud. The laundry room is on the other side of the apartment."

"I'm sure I'll be fine."

Melanie gave her one last smile before exiting, closing the door behind her. Alone at last, Spring took a few moments to center herself—but only a few. Without her coat, the cold was starting to set in. She quickly took off her earrings and the rings and bracelets she wore, then set them on the bathroom counter, doing her best not to look at her reflection. The few glimpses she caught reminded her of a wet Pomeranian. Not flattering. She had just turned to the tub, thinking through the logistics involved in washing this crap out of her hair, when the door opened behind her.

"I thought you were leaving the clothes outsi—" Her voice cut off and her eyes widened as she saw Snow standing in the doorway. The small space made him seem even bigger, especially when he turned and shut the door.

Spring's mouth went dry. Even with how rude he had been, she couldn't deny the attraction she felt. Though the room temperature seemed to rise a hundred degrees, she still shivered. She wrapped her arms around her middle and forced herself to scowl, narrowing her eyes.

"Most people knock," she said. "I could have been naked in here."

"You'd really take a shower in someone's house that you don't know?" he asked.

"Maybe." She hadn't been planning to, but she didn't like that he had figured that out about her. "What are you doing here, anyway?"

"I wanted to apologize," he said. "You thought you were helping me—"

"I *thought* I was helping you? I stopped you from being hit by a bus."

He took a deep breath, then let it out slowly. He held her gaze for a few moments, then looked her over and shook his head. Reaching up to his neck, he undid his tie and pulled it from his shirt, then opened the top few buttons. Spring felt her eyes widen again, but didn't care this time. He hung the tie on a hook behind the door, then unbuttoned his jacket and hung it up as well. A little choking noise came out of her. Somehow, he looked even bigger the more clothes he removed. And he wasn't done.

He removed his vest and hung it with the jacket and tie, then turned to her and unbuttoned the sleeves of his dark shirt. Heat exploded in her core, her skin rising in goosebumps that were intensified by the cold dampness still in her hair. She could glimpse the edges of his collarbones in the gap at his neck, and the gleaming skin of the biggest pectoral muscles she'd ever seen. He rolled up one sleeve past his elbow, then started on the other.

"Come on, you're a mess," he said. "Let's get you cleaned up."

"Excuse me?" Spring was so stunned, she just stood there as he slid past her and started up the water. It was his rudeness, his gall, and not at all that she was mesmerized by the tight pull of his pants across his backside as he bent over to check the temperature and arrange the shampoo and conditioner the way he wanted.

He turned back to her and said, "Take off your sweater."

Her heart pounded in her chest, her mouth dropping open, but only stuttering sounds emerging from it. She lifted her hands to the top button, but she wasn't sure if she wanted to do as he said or clutch the fabric to her chest.

Okay, she knew she wanted to do as he said. Then hopefully lose the rest of their clothes and jump into that shower to get each other as clean as possible. And then dirty again.

"You don't want your sweater getting messed up and wet," he said. "I know you have a chemise on under there, but I'll look away if you want."

There was something oddly comforting in the way he was speaking. His tone, his demeanor, they were so different than what she'd seen before. Aside from a slight darkening in his cheeks, there was no sign of interest in her. She'd never had a man find her so… resistible before. Again, she thought of the challenge he presented, but did she really still want to go there?

Her eyes roved over his shoulders and chest, then down his legs and back to his strong features. She absolutely still wanted to go there. But did he?

"It'll be a lot easier for me to wash your hair while you support yourself over the tub," he said. "I've done this a thousand times. You don't have anything to worry about from me."

That's what worried her. That she *didn't* have to worry about him making a move. Wait, what did he say?

"You've done this before?" Spring asked.

He shrugged. "I have girls."

The brief warm smile that accompanied the statement was so wholesome that Spring's chest filled with warmth. He was a dad? Oh crap, did that mean he had a wife or a partner? That would explain a lot. And here Spring was, lusting after him and making plans that she had no business making.

Spring turned away to try to hide her disappointment. She fumbled with the buttons of her sweater, but managed to get it off, then set it on the counter near her jewelry. Somehow, knowing that nothing was going to happen between them made her feel more vulnerable under his gaze. She was wearing a bra beneath her chemise, but she still crossed her arms over her chest when she turned back to him.

He wasn't even looking at her. He had the shower nozzle started and was pointing it toward the wall. As she approached, he gestured toward the far end of the tub, where he'd placed a stack of towels to cushion her knees as she knelt over the rim. He had even placed a folded towel over the edge of the tub to pad it there. It really did seem like he had done this before.

"I can manage on my own," she said, suddenly dreading the thought of his hands in her hair, the closeness of his body. When there had been a chance of further intimacy, this had only seemed like an appetizer. Now, it seemed totally inappropriate.

"I'm sure you can," he said, surprising her. "But it'll be a lot easier if I help."

"Are you sure your wife will be okay with that?"

He stared at her, his mouth hanging slack. Maybe she'd misread him even more than she thought.

"Husband?" she offered.

A huge smile spread across his face. Snow busted out laughing, throwing his head back. The rich sound sent a frisson of pleasure down her spine, despite her efforts to stop finding him attractive. When he finished, he shook his head and wiped a tear from his eye.

"You think I'm married?" he said. "Gods, that's funny."

"Why?" She waved her hand in his direction. "I mean you have… stuff to offer."

Wait, did he say, 'Gods,' as in plural?

His smile fell and he snapped his mouth shut, his eyebrows lowering menacingly. That muscle in his jaw twitched again. What had she done to offend him so deeply?

"Nobody's going to be jealous," he said, a bitter note to his voice. "Now, come on. Let's get this done."

Chapter Five

Spring was staring at him like a deer about to bolt. Snow had plenty of experience with that. He stepped aside, giving her space so she didn't feel threatened, and waited for her to come to him. It gave him time to get his own emotions under control.

That dig about him having a wife… It had cut deeper than he would have expected. Who the hell would want to be with him? The monster of childhood legend?

Spring didn't know he was the Krampus, though. Maybe when she looked at him, she saw… What? A viable candidate for… affection? A potential partner in life?

Those were dangerous thoughts for him to have. That echoing hollow in his chest stirred again. He wanted to rub it, to soothe the ache, but didn't dare move for fear of scaring her off. As it was, she stared at him, then the shower head in his hand, then back to him again. He tried to keep his expression as neutral as possible.

Finally, she stepped forward, then lowered herself to the towels he'd provided. She braced herself with her hands on the base of the tub, then turned to face the wall away from him so that the water wouldn't get in her eyes.

Or so that she wouldn't have to look at him. He had plenty of experience with that, too. Not so much since the Winter Queen had given him his new forms, but still. Things like that were hard to forget.

He lowered himself to one knee behind Spring, keeping his other leg bent so he could rise easily if needed, and tried to let as little of their bodies touch as he could. The water was a good temperature, but he was still careful to watch her response as he started to rinse her hair. The golden strands were caked with road dirt from the slush.

He hated that she'd put herself through this for no reason. He would have been fine, though she hadn't known that. For the first time, he realized the danger she had placed herself in—for him. No one had ever done anything like that before. The feeling of hollowness in his chest retreated a little, warmth filling the space instead.

He didn't have to help bathe his children often, but sometimes, there were kids who would act out with their caretakers in the Yuletide Kingdom, and Snow would have to step in to make sure neither they nor any other members of his court were injured. Most of the children had seen him in his polar bear form when he came to take them as tribute to the Winter Queen. They weren't as likely to lash out at Snow as his other subjects. And though he could use his magic to clean them, they needed to learn to care for themselves and let others care for them. Plus, nobody he had met liked the chilling experience of being cleaned with snow-based magic.

Washing Spring's hair was not at all like helping his kids. Physically, the motions were similar, but she was bigger than they were for a start. It was hard not to bump against her as he held the shower head close to her hair. Running his fingers over the strands to coax out the dirt was different, too. The warmth in his chest spread lower, his skin prickling with the awareness of her proximity.

He often used stories to distract the more ornery kids he tended back in the Yuletide Kingdom. This time, maybe he could distract himself. He just had to be careful not to let anything slip that would make Spring suspect he was anything other than a mortal man.

"I had this kid named Malachi," he began. "When he came to us, he was a mess. I don't know what he'd gotten himself into, and I honestly don't want to know. But he had layers of grime, and he refused to let anyone bathe him. I don't think he'd ever had a bath in his life. He was too young to leave on his own safely, and he was such a spitfire. Gertrude, one of the women assigned to care for him, came to me and asked me to help her."

Snow set aside the shower head where it wouldn't spray Spring and picked up the shampoo, working it into a rich lather as he spoke, making himself focus on the memory and not the soft texture of her hair sliding between his fingers.

"The smell was just... incredible," Snow said. "We had the tub all ready with plenty of warm water, fresh, clean clothes laid out for him, plus toys and towels. This little four-year-old boy stood there, arms crossed over his filthy clothes, glaring at me like he was ready to take me down while Gertrude was just shaking her head in the background." Snow chuckled as he lost himself deeper in the memory, rinsing the suds from Spring's hair till the water was clear, then started working conditioner through the golden strands.

"What happened?" Spring prompted.

"Well... He did."

She twisted around a bit so that she could look him in the face, her eyebrows high on her forehead. Snow laughed at her expression as much as the memory.

"Malachi was the first child I helped under my... current boss," Snow said. "I had no idea what I was doing. Figured I could pick him up and dump him into the tub, clothes and all." He chuckled louder as he rinsed out the conditioner in her hair. "That kid clawed his way up my arms like a housecat. Made it all the way onto my shoulders and jumped off. I was kind of off balance to start, so I fell into the tub headfirst."

Spring started to laugh. The sound brought a deeper smile to Snow's face. He turned off the water and squeezed the excess moisture from her hair, then reached for a towel as they both rose to their feet.

"The joke was on him, though," Snow said, placing the towel on her head and starting to gently dry it.

"Why?"

"When I hit the water, I splashed so much out of the tub that Malachi was drenched from standing there next to it. We sort of stared at each other for a minute, and then we both busted out laughing. He was still holding his sides when I sloshed my way out of the room to let Gertrude take over."

"And that's the same Malachi I heard you talking to North about?"

Snow thought back over their conversation. Had they said anything they shouldn't have within earshot of a mortal? Snow wasn't used to giving mortals any consideration beyond what he needed to keep his operations in the mortal realm running. At the same time, he couldn't bring himself to outright lie to her.

"It is," Snow said. "He's grown now, into a fine man. Helps me run everything."

"Ah." Spring nodded, an odd glittering in her eyes. "So, you work in a place that takes care of kids? Like an orphanage?"

"It's closer to foster care. They stay with us forever and learn to contribute to our realm."

Crap, did mortals talk like that? If Spring had thought it an odd turn of phrase, she didn't act like it. She was still staring up at him, her eyes a little glassy.

"You give them a home," she said.

"Exactly."

How was it that this mortal understood his mission when North had totally lost sight of it? As the Yule Cat and the Krampus, the pair of them had been responsible for bringing new people into the Yuletide Kingdom for almost more years than Snow could remember. They selected children who were neglected or abused, who weren't getting the love and care that all children deserved.

So what if the Yuletide Kingdom had been locked in winter for as long as they had been working together. Their ruler was called the Winter Queen for a reason. But now, North had it in his head that their realm wasn't good enough, just because the weather never changed. Snow looked into Spring's eyes and more of that warmth bloomed in his chest. Was North right? Did the Yuletide Kingdom need to bring back spring and all that came with it to infuse the realm with love once more?

Snow knew the seasons used to come and go with as much regularity as in any other Faerie Kingdom. He didn't know why winter had come and suddenly never ended, but it was right around the time that the Winter Queen had brought him and North into her Court and made them Fairy Lords. Around the time that Lord Kringle had been banished to the farthest reaches of her realm.

When the Winter Queen had found Snow, he had been trapped in the mishappen form of the Krampus, with curving horns sticking out from his head and goat legs. He had still tried help people, as naive as that had been. One look at him, and they'd all run in terror. He wondered what Spring would think of his original form. The thought of her running from him brought a sharp, stabbing pain to his chest.

She stared up at him, her large blue eyes wide and shimmering with moisture. Had some water reached them when he was wrapped up in his story? He needed to be more careful. She was mortal, after all. He lightened his touch further as he worked to dry her hair.

Her lips parted slightly, working noiselessly for a few moments before she said, "I think… I think I've got it."

Her voice was rough and she coughed to clear it. Then she reached up and placed her hands on his, halting their motion.

The skin of her hands was impossibly soft, their warmth soaking into him so quickly, it was almost as if he'd been scalded. At the same time, electric awareness coursed through him, his chest lit up with an energy powerful enough he was shocked he wasn't glowing from it. She pulled his hands away from her head, clutching them tightly.

Did she feel the same pull that he did? The same strange energy connecting them? He wanted to ask, but… What if she didn't? And even if she did, would she feel the same if she knew that he was the Krampus?

Before he could pull away himself, she released his hands and stepped back, staring downward as she swallowed hard. The distance she placed between them felt like a wedge driven into his heart. She tugged the towel off her soaked hair and held it in front of her.

"If you don't mind, I'd like a moment to myself to finish up," she said. She cast a quick glance at him, but her eyes narrowed almost as if it pained her to look at him. She quickly looked away.

"Yeah, sure." He stiffened, pulling the door open and striding from the room without looking back. He yanked it shut behind him.

Why was this different? Why did her rejection hurt so much worse than all the other times people had turned him away? He headed for the staircase, eager to leave. When he reached the foyer, he realized he had left his jacket in the bathroom with Spring. And with it, his phone, his wallet, his keys…

He could get around without them and even gain access to his offices, but doing so would risk people witnessing his magic. And his phone… Who could get by without their phone in the mortal realm anymore? Growling low, he turned toward the living room, pacing back and forth in the small space. Small for him, anyway.

He heard movement behind him. His heart did a funny little flip in his chest, his stomach fluttering as he turned around, expecting Spring. Melanie stood there, holding

Spring's red coat. She let out a yelp and jumped back.

"Snow? What are you doing here?"

What *was* he doing here? He'd come to apologize. And he had sort of done that. He had stayed to help Spring. To spend time with her. The way she'd spoken to him before had riled him up in a way no one else ever had. Then again, no one had ever tried. She had *flirted* with him. With *him*.

"I don't even know," he said.

Melanie looked back and forth between him and the closed door to the bathroom. A smile slowly crept across her face.

"Wait, did you come up here to apologize?" she said.

"What? No." He shook his head, then said, "I mean, yeah. Maybe."

Melanie pinched her lips between her teeth, something he'd noticed that she did when she didn't want to say something or show how excited she was. If she thought something was brewing between Spring and Snow, she was going to be disappointed, and Snow couldn't allow that.

"Don't make that face," he said.

"What face?" She pointed at her chin. "This face?"

The smile she was barely suppressing flooded over her features. More warmth fluttered in Snow's chest. Not the kind that soaked into his bones, such as Spring had started to bring out of him, but a gentler warmth.

"What are you doing up here?" Snow asked. "The bakery is busier than I've ever seen it."

"The new cookie recipes North and I came up with are really popular, aren't they?" Melanie said, crossing the room to stand in front of him. "I always wanted to be a baker. Working here, living here, everything that's happened, it's better than a dream come true."

"I'm glad." Despite the weight in his own heart, he couldn't help but be happy for her. He looked down at the red coat that Melanie held, forgotten in her hands. A dark gray stain covered half the fabric. "What the heck are you doing to that coat?"

"I'm cleaning it," Melanie said, her smile dimming a bit. "Trying to, anyway. I've never been good at this kind of stuff."

He looked over her head at the bathroom door to make sure it was still shut, then said, "Give it here."

Melanie looked over her shoulder, then turned back to him and smiled, nodding eagerly. She handed him the coat, her eyes wide with wonder as she waited for him to work his magic—literally. Snow shook his head, but he couldn't help but smile at her.

He held the coat up by its shoulders with both hands. A light, floral scent emanated from it. Of course, Spring would smell like flowers. He chuckled as he worked his magic into the fibers, the remaining liquid stiffening as it froze. The fabric crackled as he gave it a shake, gray snow falling to the ground from the areas that had been saturated with slush. He shook it again and again, till the snow he was pushing through the fibers came out white. As she critically checked the now-clean coat, Melanie's smile broadened—until she saw the pile of snow on the floor beneath it.

"Oh crap," she said. "I'll go get a towel."

"No need." He stomped his foot in the center of the mess. Snowflakes swirled out from beneath his boot, sweeping up everything that had dropped onto the floor and carrying it a few feet into the air in a whirlwind before vanishing.

"That is so cool," she said, her eyes wide.

"The coolest." He winked at her as he folded Spring's coat over his arm. "I'll take it from here."

"But don't you want me to deal with her when—"

He reached out and grasped Melanie's arm gently, giving it a squeeze. Slowly, he repeated. "I'll take it from here. You can head back down and help out North in the bakery."

"Okay." Her lips pinched together as she tried to hold in her smile again and utterly failed. Rising on her tip-toes, she planted a quick kiss on his cheek, then hurried from the room, casting a last glance at him over her shoulder as her smile finally emerged, completely free.

Snow shook his head as he heard the door to the apartment shut behind her. North was definitely going to tease him about this. Snow had no doubt that the pair would be speculating about what was going on upstairs. Snow was speculating about that himself.

Spring had seemed interested in him. Aggressively so. But, when he'd left her just now, she was different. Quieter. More subdued. Maybe his help hadn't been as welcome as he'd thought it might be. Maybe she didn't like his story or didn't like kids. That would be a total dealbreaker. Snow's life revolved around the people he brought into the Yuletide kingdom—the children who grew to be members of his household. Anyone who wanted to be with him would have to understand that.

Was that what he wanted? To be with her? Somehow, a glimmer of hope was burgeoning within him that maybe she felt that way about him, but... Maybe she wasn't interested. If she knew who he really was, she wouldn't want to be with him at all. She would run away, as had so many others.

This was stupid. He had other things to do. Important things. People to take care of. He draped her coat over the back of one of the stuffed chairs, but couldn't bring himself to leave. His jacket and vest were still in the bathroom. That's why he was lingering. Not because he wanted to see her once more before she walked out of his life forever.

A low growl built in the back of his throat. He didn't want her to walk out of his life. He kept his hand resting on the chair, feeling the rough wool of her coat. What was it about this woman that was drawing him in?

The door to the bathroom opened and Spring emerged. Snow's heartbeat picked up and his mouth went dry. His fingers curled into the fabric of her coat and his breath quickened. She had dried her hair as much as she could, but it hung in tight strands around her face, darkened from the water that remained in it. She stared at him with those same wide eyes as before. Almost fearful, but not quite. Why was he suddenly making her nervous now?

He hated the idea of her being afraid of him. A crushing pressure seized his heart at the thought, as if it were in a vise. Where was the smirk that drove him crazy? Where were the innuendos that set him spinning? He wanted to bring those out of her again.

This was a challenge he wouldn't back down from. He wasn't the Krampus anymore. He was the Lord of Endless Snow. This woman had been happy to interact with him just moments ago. He would make that happen again. Somehow…

Chapter Six

He is way too dangerous.

Spring wrapped her arms around her middle, wishing she'd worn a thicker sweater, even if it didn't match the holiday. This was turning into the worst Valentine's Day ever. Moisture clung to the fibers of the garment, chilling her almost as badly as her damp hair. She knew she shouldn't go out like this, but it would be worse to stay here—with him.

Snow stood across the room, his dark shirt unbuttoned enough to give her a mouth-watering view of the best chest she'd ever seen. Smooth, gold-tinged skin stretched across massive pecs. One fist was propped on his hip while the other gripped the back of a chair, giving her an excellent view of the shape of his enormous back. With his sleeves rolled up past his elbows, she could see the corded muscles of his forearms.

She'd felt those strong arms around her. Not in the passionate way she'd originally intended. No, he had held her with such tenderness and care that her heart was still flopping in her chest like a fish out of water. He had told her that wonderful story. Shared that he was already living her dream—helping as many children as possible in the best way he could.

He stared at her with such intensity she would have sworn his eyes had a faint red glow to their dark depths, like the embers of an endless fire. But she had no idea if it was because he was as attracted to her as she was to him or that she was still driving him crazy—the annoying kind of crazy, not the sexy kind she had hoped for. Certainly not… Not the forever kind. Not the first flutters of love.

She realized that one hand had gone up to her heart, covering it as if that could keep it in her chest. As if that could stop its longing for him and keep her safe. Physical stuff could happen fast, and she was fine with that. But this? She was falling too hard and too fast. She shook her head sharply, breaking her gaze away from his. She had to get out of here.

"Thanks for washing my hair," she said.

He chuckled, the low sound rumbling across the room to her like distant thunder. Her eyes snapped back to him despite herself. He ran his hand over his dark, close-cropped hair.

"Maybe someday you'll be able to return the favor," he said.

Her lip twitched into an almost-smile, drawing his gaze. Why was he staring at her mouth with that intense look, his eyes narrowing and his shoulders squared? She needed him to go back to being perplexed and annoyed. This predatory scrutiny made her feel as if she needed to run. The trouble was, she was pretty sure if she did, it would be straight into his arms.

A shiver racked her and she hugged herself tighter. Her coat was right next to him. Too close to him. She could take her chances with the cold. Except, when the tremor passed through her, he hissed in a breath. He shook his head as he stood straighter, then stalked across the room toward her. Her eyes widened with each step he took, her breath quickening and tingles spreading through her body.

What was he going to do? Was he going to kiss her? To lift her from her feet so she could wrap her legs around his waist as he tore his way through her clothes so he could bury himself deep? Her core clenched at the thought, a shocking burst of pleasure throbbing out through her body. No one had ever made her feel like this, and he hadn't even touched her.

When he reached her, he didn't stop moving. He swept her up off her feet, but not as she'd imagined. Instead, he lifted her into his arms. She gasped at the momentary sensation of weightlessness as he practically threw her into the air. Gravity reasserted itself, settling her against his chest. She felt so perfect against him. It was as if she was meant to be there.

"Wh—what are you doing?" she asked as he turned back toward the couch.

"Getting you warmed up."

She was already warmed up—practically on fire wanting him. He strode to the couch. That would work, too. It was a big couch. Well, for her. He was so huge, she wondered how he would fit. It would be better if he set her on the faux fur rug in front of the fire. Instead, he strode up to the back of the couch… and dropped her over it.

She bounced on the cushions a few times, staring up at him in shock. He picked up the blanket draped over the couch and unfolded it, snapping it in the air once above to spread it fully, then let it fall over her. This was really not going the way she'd expected. Snow reached one long arm over the back of the couch and bent down behind it. What was he doing now?

Gravity seemed to stop working for a moment again as he lifted her, couch and all, and started walking toward the fireplace. Her mind reeled with a mix of frustration and excitement. How strong was this guy? As he set the very large couch down only a few feet from the fire's protective screen, she caught a glimpse of his face. There was no sign of strain whatsoever.

"Okay," he said, staring down at her with his fists on his hips. "Better?"

"What?" she gasped.

He gestured toward the fire, then toward her. "The fire. The blanket. You were cold."

She had been so focused on what he was doing, she

hadn't had a chance to really think of the 'why' behind it. Now that she knew… It was really sweet, in a super sexy, how-the-heck-did-he-do-that kind of way. This guy was a heady mix of contradictions, and he was hitting all the right buttons with her.

She shook herself inwardly. Nobody pushed her buttons. Not the emotional ones, anyway. Not anymore. She had learned her lesson too many times. She needed to go back to just seeing him as a fun diversion. A Valentine's Day challenge to have a little fun with, and then they could both move on. She arched an eyebrow at him and pulled the blanket closer around her neck.

"I don't know," she said. "I'm still pretty cold. Maybe you could help me warm up." She cast her best sultry smile at him.

He nodded, then started walking past the back of the couch. "I'll get more blankets."

"Wait." Spring let out a frustrated gasp. She grabbed his arm as soon as he was within reach. "That's not what I meant."

He stared down at her hand on him, dark eyebrows drawn over his forehead. His eyes traveled slowly up her arm and over her shoulder, leaving a wake of goosebumps as it did. She could swear she felt his gaze like a caress. It lingered on her lips and a muscle in his clenched jaw started to twitch. Her breath picked up again, her heart pounding in her chest. Their eyes locked, and the longing deep within his eyes seared her to her soul.

She could barely breathe. Her fingers tightened around his arm, her back arching as if her entire body was straining toward him. He felt like gravity, and she wanted to fall into him, even though she was terrified. Because when she stared into his eyes, she felt a mirror of that longing within herself.

He wasn't just a conquest—no matter how hard she tried to fool herself into thinking so. Somehow, she knew… he was her *forever*.

Snow gently placed his hand over hers, his strong fingers wrapping around it and detaching her grip. He held on, though, his head bowed.

"I'm not that kind of guy," he said.

"What kind of guy?" she echoed. "The kind with a gruff exterior, but who's caring and kind beneath? The kind who's cold and bitter at first, but when you get down to it, actually sweet? Did you even see the beverage I was drinking in the bakery?"

He chuckled, but wouldn't look at her. He squeezed her hand one more time, then said, "I'll get you those blankets."

"Snow—"

She stopped speaking as the lights cut out abruptly. The fireplace went dark as well, and a biting cold swept through the room. She clung to Snow's hand, not even able to see any light from the windows. What was going on?

Once again, gravity felt like it couldn't decide what was up and what was down, but this time, it was an entirely unpleasant experience. Her stomach lurched as she fell up off the couch, her wet hair was rising around her face, then falling along with the rest of her.

She landed against a warm chest, shivering violently as her breath came out in clouds. At first, it was all she could see, but then Snow emerged, as if he'd been wrapped in a darkness that was retreating from his form. It seemed to merge with the inky blackness surrounding them.

"What's g-going on?" she asked, though chattering teeth.

"I'm not sure." Snow pulled her closer against his chest, wrapping his arms around her and giving her what warmth he could. It wasn't enough.

"I'm f-freezing," she said, the cold burning her even through her clothes. "H-how are you st-still w-warm?"

He bent over her, as if trying to shield her from the cold with his body. Her hair crackled as she burrowed against Snow's chest. The lingering dampness in it had already frozen.

"H-how l-long t-till I g-get f-frostbite?" It wouldn't be long, with her icy hair against her ears.

"Frost," he hissed under his breath.

"W-what?"

"Frost!" he yelled, searching the darkness around them.

"Better do something quick." A man's voice came from

somewhere—from everywhere—in the void, sing-songy and mocking.

"Dammit." Snow looked down at her. The reddish glow in his eyes was back, distorted and bright through the crystals of frost coating her eyelashes. "I'm sorry."

He took a deep breath and stood straighter. She whimpered as his warmth retreated, but then a blast of cold radiated out from his chest making her shudder. The cold wrapped around her, touching every part of her skin. Instead of burning, it tingled, sending goosebumps over her flesh. She looked down to see a swirl of snowflakes whirling around her body, penetrating her clothes and flooding them with light.

The snowflakes swept up past her face, racing over her scalp and down her hair, drying it and pulling it up on the sides with what felt like combs. The rest tumbled down her back and around her neck, warming her. She felt something rest across her forehead and a light weight on her ears as if she had put on a heavier set of earrings. The cold that had been biting her vanished, her eyes clearing as the frost disappeared from her eyelashes.

The snow brightened around her body as her thin red sweater and woolen skirt expanded to a rich velvet dress of burnished gold, inset with satin as bright as rays of morning sunlight in complex patterns of ivy and flowers. Though the dress showed off a lovely amount of her cleavage, the cold raced away as a platinum necklace formed around her neck, the metal channel set with diamonds and suspending a bright golden-yellow citrine as big as an egg that nestled just above her breasts. She felt more jewelry form on her fingers, but didn't dare let go of Snow to look at it.

Snow's grip on her waist tightened, his breath hitching as he pulled her closer. Beneath the skirts of the dress, her tights turned into something that felt like the softest, warmest fleece she'd ever encountered, brushing against her skin in a tantalizing wave of warmth, almost as if someone's hand roved over it. She gasped as she felt her undergarments shift and change, the silky fabric whispering over her skin in the most intimate of places.

Snow let out a low, rumbling growl, bending closer. Heat bloomed in her stomach, quickly spreading to the rest of her and chasing away the last of the aching cold. She wrapped her arms around his neck, pulling herself up till their lips were a hair's breadth apart. Just before they touched, that annoying voice intruded on the moment.

"*That's* the kind of guy he is," it said.

Chapter Seven

Snow held Spring tightly in his arms. He never wanted to let her go. He wanted... He wanted all kinds of things. Things he had never considered before. His skin was on fire where they touched, and his lips were tingling with the urge to kiss her. His cock was harder than he'd thought possible, straining against his pants as if trying to reach her. Oh, what he wanted to do to her with it... From the heat in her eyes, the warmth of her body he could sense pooling low in her belly, he was sure she wanted the same. But first, he had to deal with Jack Frost.

Snow straightened, keeping Spring secure against his side. He didn't dare release her, with them being stuck in a pocket of Faerie that Frost had created around them. If Frost tried to spirit her away... Snow's shoulder's bunched, his bear form pushing against him, urging him to change so that he could more effectively protect her, could kill Frost faster. But if she saw Snow change...

The thought doused his ardor, sending something over his skin he almost never felt—a chill. She knew he wasn't a regular mortal now. Maybe she could accept that he was a Fairy Lord and even that he was a magic-wielding shapeshifter. But what would she think if she knew of his original form? Would she still let him touch her? Hold her? Would she still look at him with heavy-lidded eyes as if she wanted to kiss him as much as he wanted to kiss her?

Frost had done this. He had forced Snow to blow his cover and reveal himself—breaking the most sacred law of all Fae. Snow would have been expected to let her die, but he couldn't. Just the thought almost broke his control, snow ghosting up from his skin as if asking if it was time to transform.

"Frost, I am going to snap you in half," Snow growled.

"Why would you want to do that?" Frost said, his voice cloyingly sweet. "After I've been so kind and given you two your own private paradise."

In a blink, the darkness around them vanished, leaving them in a small cabin. Snow looked around, taking in the huge fireplace with its natural stone, the smooth-polished oak floors, the stairs hugging one wall leading up to a loft, and the kitchen island separating that part of the great room from the living area. He knew this place. He also knew the smarmy dickweed who was leaning against the wall near the fireplace.

Jack Frost stood with his arms crossed over his chest, his dark eyebrows lowered over ice blue eyes and his black hair a carefully crafted 'mess.' His lips were pulled into a condescending smirk that Snow wanted to punch off his face.

"You teleported us," Snow said. "This is Sylvia's cabin."

"Sylvia's cabin?" Frost leaned forward, a guileless expression crossing his face that Snow didn't believe for a second. "You mean the place where you betrayed your Queen and used the power that was rightfully mine to turn some deer guy and his girlfriend into the Lord and Lady of the North Wind? That cabin?"

"Frost," Snow growled in warning.

Frost pushed himself away from the wall, strolling closer to the fire. He snapped his fingers in front of it, and a raging blaze appeared from out of nowhere.

"We wouldn't want dear Spring to get chilly," Frost said. "Mortals are so sensitive to the cold and all."

"You are way over the line." Snow took a step closer.

Frost laughed, his form turning to cold vapor that hung in the air for a moment, then dropped to the ground. A chill breeze swept through the cabin as he flew across the room. He reformed in the hallway that led to the outer door of the cabin.

"You know, I think you should have opened up a bit more with your student," Frost said. "He could have given you tips on some much more entertaining ways to help a mortal woman stay warm, as he and Sylvia did their first night together. Right here in front of this fire."

Snow stiffened, his legs refusing to obey him as the implications of Frost's words sank in. Spring didn't have the same problem.

"Oh my God, you perv," she shouted. "Did you watch them?"

"Of course not." Frost rolled his eyes and snorted. "How bored do you think I am, that I would peep on a couple in the intense throes of passion?" His voice became mockingly dramatic toward the end of his sentence.

"Well, you're bored enough to mess with us," Spring said. "And that chill you sent my way was no joke."

"It wasn't meant as one," he snapped. "Your lover boy here was entrusted with a sacred power after his bestie decided to go off the rails and desert his post. North Cotter? He's the Yule Cat." She laughed, but Frost just went on. "Not going to believe that when you're hearing it straight from Jack Frost?" He whirled his finger in a circle, making a tiny cyclone of ice crystals that vanished along with her smile.

"The Winter Queen ordered Snow to give that power to me. But instead, he gave it to his little deer pal, Aidan, and his mortal girlfriend, Sylvia."

"Wait, Aidan and Sylvia from the bakery?" Spring said, glancing over at Snow. "I've chatted with them before."

"They're the White Stag and the White Doe." Snow's voice was low and somber. She knew so much already, it seemed better to tell her everything.

"Oh, wow," she said, her eyes widening. "I've really stumbled into something, haven't I?"

"Their power was meant to be mine," Frost cut back in. "But just because Mr. Control Freak here couldn't let go of his best friend, the Yule Cat, he decided to give it to someone else."

"Wow, I can't imagine why." Spring's voice dripped with sarcasm. "I mean, you seem like such a nice and stable person. Absolutely, the best choice for so much power."

Snow snorted, his chuckle turning into a genuine laugh at the outraged expression on Frost's face. Frost barely spared Spring a glance.

"It must eat you up inside, knowing you can't get to your precious protégés, 'the Lord and Lady of the North Wind.'" Frost pushed an impressive amount of contempt into his voice.

"Aidan and Sylvia will do fine," Snow said. "And I'll be able to help them in person eventually."

"Eventually." Frost scoffed. "Unless the Queen decides this little time-out in the mortal realm you're in should be permanent."

Snow tried to hide how much the thought of that worried him. He wasn't sure how successful he was, but Frost was off on a different tangent, it seemed.

"That little trick of yours, turning a mortal into a Fae to get around our rules, only works once, even for a little suck-up like you," Frost said. "Especially since you don't have any spare power to give anyone now. Unless, of course, you decide to make Spring here the Lady of Endless Snow."

A wave of unease swept down Snow's spine. The cruel look on Frost's face just made it worse. He made a tutting sound, his eyebrows furrowed as if he was thinking hard on something.

"But wait, if you gave her your power, that would mean you wouldn't be the Lord of Endless Snow anymore," Frost said. "You'd just be plain old *Krampus*."

Snow's skin erupted in tingling prickles, as if he'd rolled in stinging nettles. His bear pushed at his flesh, begging to be let loose to rip Frost to shreds. But if Snow did that, he was certain to frighten Spring. He couldn't handle the thought of her looking at him as if he was a monster. But if she knew what the Krampus was... then it was already too late.

"Krampus?" Spring asked, her head angled as if she was trying to remember something. "Why does that sound familiar?"

Frost's smug smile sent more dread tearing through Snow. He lurched forward, arms snapping together to grab Frost and squeeze him till he stopped talking. Frost dropped his corporeal form again, and Snow was left coated in a thin layer of frost. The annoying Fae reformed above the mantle this time, lounging along its length.

"I have to run," he said. "But to answer your question, he is the Krampus." Frost nodded toward Snow. "You probably didn't recognize him in his new form, so let me help you out with that before I go."

"Frost," Snow roared.

The other Fae smiled, his face was twisted in a cruel mockery of mirth. A thick layer of frost formed over his body, the tiny crystals morphing into a visage Snow hoped he would never see again. That long, sharp nose and matching chin were too familiar, even in this terrible ice-sculpture, as were the long, curving horns that rose straight from the top of his head. His lower body morphed into the cloven-hooved goatlike legs that Snow had hobbled on for so long. A sinewy tail made of ice with a tufted end flicked once, and then the entire thing crumbled in on itself, the ephemeral frost it was made of vanishing in a puff of steam before the fire.

Snow couldn't move. He couldn't breathe. All he could do was relive the moments when he had been trapped in that form and remember people running from him, screaming. Using darkness to mask his appearance as he tried to help others, and always—*always*—being found out for who he was and met with revulsion. Mist rose from his skin, swirling around him as his polar bear form burst forth in a blinding flash of radiance.

His heart was pounding, his mind filled with rage. The windows shook as he roared, the force of it extinguishing the fire and coating the walls before him in a thick coat of snow. He would destroy the walls holding him in this small space, then find Frost and rip him to shreds. He lifted one white-furred arm, ready to smash through a window, when he felt a small hand on his elbow. Breathing heavily, he paused and turned to see who dared try to keep him from his prey.

Spring stood next to him, eyebrows drawn together in worry. Her lips were parted, and a look of such compassion was on her face that it extinguished his anger instantly. She dared to move closer as he held himself still and pressed her other hand on his chest above his heart.

"Don't let Frost manipulate you," she said. "Show me the kind of man you truly are. Stay with me."

He let his bear form drop from him like a cloak, snow circling him in a whirlwind, then expanding out to restore the room to the way it had been. He added more of his own magic to it, summoning a glowing fire in the hearth, then expanded the sphere to create a bubble around the cabin that would shield them from any prying eyes—even those of the Fae. When he was done, he stared into Spring's eyes, his chest still heaving, his heart filled with more uncertainty than he'd ever known.

How could she want him now? He braced himself for her rejection. Instead she stared at him with that assessing look of hers. The moments dragged on in silence.

"I remember the stories now," she said. "The ones I

heard about the Krampus."

He clenched his jaw, lips pressed in a thin line. There had been many places she could have started this conversation. How he had made her gown, his powers as Lord of Endless Snow, Jack Frost and their history. But she had gone straight to the topic that could hurt him most.

"The children you're fostering…" she said. "You take them, don't you? Those are the 'naughty' children from the tales."

It felt as though she'd punched him in his chest. He had thought his being the Krampus would be the most painful topic they could discuss, but she was going after his relationship with his kids? He drew himself up taller, hands curling into fists.

"I take the unwanted," he said. "The broken and forgotten. I give them purpose. Teach them to channel their anger and pain. I bring them to the Yuletide Kingdom and present them to the Winter Queen to give them a home. To give them a chance to be part of something instead of always being on the outside. Always alone."

She was quiet for a long time. Was she watching him squirm? Could she see that there was still a glimmer of hope within him? Always that stupid hope—back when he'd been the Krampus, and even now, looking at this beautiful woman and realizing just how much he already cared what she thought of him. He should never have let this happen.

"Frost is wrong," she said. "I don't think you're a control freak. No, I think what you do is all about fear."

"Fear?" Snow said, a laugh bursting from him despite their situation. He pounded a fist on his chest, then stepped closer so that he was hovering over her. A little frisson of awareness shot up his spine at how close they were, but he shoved it away. "I am the terrifying Krampus. What do I have to fear?"

She didn't back down or even cringe. In fact, she leaned closer to him. The frisson turned to heat that entered through his chest and pooled deep in his belly. The fire in her eyes could melt all the snow in the universe.

"It isn't about control," she reiterated. "It's about caring. You care so much for your loved ones, you're terrified something will happen to them and you'll lose them. That's why you want everyone in their place, everyone doing the tasks you think will keep them safest. That's why you couldn't let North go and why it's bothering you so much that you're unable to get to Aidan and Sylvia."

The heat in his chest instantly chilled at her words, dread taking its place as his imagination filled in the details of what she suggested. The Winter Queen could be so cold, even to those in her court. Look at how she had exiled North so abruptly—and then made it permanent. Just because he wasn't the Lord of the North Wind anymore didn't mean he wasn't interested in visiting their home, the people that he had helped raise from the time they were young.

Snow couldn't imagine being cut off from his people so completely—his children. He couldn't even think of his own pseudo-exile becoming permanent without changing back to his polar bear form and destroying the cabin. Sure, he'd trained his people well enough that they could keep things running without him, but he didn't want them to. The only thing keeping him from going completely crazy was that his holdings in the mortal realm gave him a conduit to his operations in the Kingdom of the Yuletide Fae.

He hated being cut off from his people. He hated that North wasn't standing at his side anymore. He hated that he couldn't support and guide Aidan and Sylvia as they got their bearings. Most of all, he hated that this mortal had laid this all out so plainly in front of him that he couldn't ignore it anymore.

"Stop talking," Snow growled.

Spring snorted, then stepped even closer to him, their chests almost brushing as she craned her neck back to fiercely hold his attention.

"You're afraid they'll mess up and need you and you won't be able to get to them in time," she said.

"Stop talking." His stomach twisted at the thought. What would make this infuriating mortal stop flinging these painful truths at him?

"You're not trying to control everyone, you're trying to keep them all safe."

He grabbed her arms and practically lifted her from her feet as he crushed his mouth to hers in a searing kiss. It hadn't been thought out, it had been instinct that made him reach for her. Self-preservation. But once his lips touched hers, something new burst forth in his chest. A need, a desire, so fierce that it consumed him.

His reason fled, his own self-control vanished, and all he knew was Spring. Her heat. Her arms twisting free from his grasp only to wrap around his neck and pull him closer, deepening their kiss. Snow groaned as his tongue slid into the velvet wetness of her mouth, her own there to greet him in a sparring dance. His cock sprang to life, straining against his pants and sending arcs of pleasure through him. She raked her fingernails lightly across his scalp, demanding more. He would give her everything he had. Everything he was.

Chapter Eight

Spring had been certain that Snow was filled with passion under his carefully controlled veneer. She had not been wrong. He kissed her as if he were drowning and she was air. As if she was his… everything. She was starting to feel the same toward him, even with all that she'd learned, all that she was still trying to reconcile in her mind.

He was powerful. He was magical. He could transform and had been transformed. It would take time for those aspects of his nature to feel truly real. But what already felt real, what she knew in her heart, was that he was a good man. The best she'd ever met. And he was her match, no matter how he'd started out or what the future held.

She deepened the kiss, heat spreading through her body, demanding more. More of his hands on her, more contact. The stupid—gorgeous—dress made it hard for them to get closer, with its full skirts. How was she supposed to get it off? He had made it with magic. Did it even have a zipper or a clasp?

She kissed her way along his epic jawline, distracted by the pine and crisp snow scent of him. How could someone smell like freshly fallen snow? Her skin raced with goosebumps, confused by the invigorating scent and the warmth he was wrapping her in. Tabling that for later, she finally reached his ear, sucking his earlobe between her teeth and gently raking them over the sensitive skin.

His hands clutched her back as he hissed in a breath, pressing her harder against him. She couldn't wait to get her hands on the impressive bulge prodding her stomach, but would force herself to. She needed more mobility to do all the things she wanted.

Releasing his ear, she nuzzled his neck and said, "Can you maybe help me with this dress?"

"What do you need?" he rasped, his voice even deeper than usual.

She chuckled and nipped his ear again. "I need to take it off."

His hands twitched against her back, his grip on her tightening. For a moment, she feared he was going to just tear the gorgeous dress off of her. And what about the clothing she'd been wearing before? That was her favorite Valentine's Day outfit.

"Can you change it back?" she asked.

"You don't like it?" He pulled back a bit, and the doubt in his eyes tugged at her heart.

She reached up and stroked his cheek. "I love it. But I don't know how to manage it. You can dress me up again later. Right now, I'm more interested in getting undressed."

A low growl rumbled out from his chest. The fire behind him roared higher, heat flooding the room. It was a good thing, because a moment later, snowflakes enveloped her, sweeping across her clothing and turning everything back to the way it had been before. Her hair was still dry, thankfully.

Somehow, being in her familiar clothes made everything that had happened seem more real. She was still herself, not some princess swept into a fairytale. But Snow… He was definitely her prince.

He bent to reclaim her lips, kissing her as if that momentary pause had starved him. His tongue dominated hers, both begging and demanding. She met his need, his passion with her own. She longed to leap up and wrap her legs around his waist, but her skirt was still too long. Releasing his neck, she reached down to unzip her skirt, wanting to be rid of it.

He grabbed her hand, lightning-quick, bringing it to his waist. Apparently, he was still working through his control issues. Spring didn't mind. She trusted him. He reached between them and quickly unfastened the buttons of her sweater, pulling the soft fabric down her arms and holding it there as he moved his kisses to her neck. The heat pouring through her where they touched turned to lava, flooding her body, pooling deep in her belly and lighting up her core.

With her arms pinned at her sides, he took his time nipping and nuzzling and kissing her neck, tantalizing the skin. She shimmied against him, wanting to be closer, wanting to hold him, to touch him. He returned his kisses to her lips as he pulled her sweater down farther, but kept it at her wrists, clasping them against her back with one huge hand as the other went to her breast. She gasped against his mouth as he squeezed the tender flesh. Her core throbbed in time with his movements as he rolled her nipple with his thumb.

Growling, he released her arms and mouth, finally pulling her sweater off of her and flinging it away. He dropped to his knees before her, holding her waist as he captured one breast, then the other with his mouth, flicking her nipple with his tongue through the silky fabric of her chemise. She gasped again, clasping his head against her chest as the conflagration flowing through her threatened to melt her knees.

He dipped his hands under her chemise, hands cool against her burning skin, and ran them up to cup her breasts as he worked her nipples through her bra. The throbbing ache between her legs intensified. Her need for him was driving her crazy. She'd never wanted anyone like this before.

He rose, taking the chemise with him and tossing it aside. She glanced down to see that he had left her bra—and it wasn't the one she'd put on that morning. Soft gold lace in a demi-cup held up her breasts in an excellent balance of support and display. The lace had a pattern of hearts and snowflakes, the perfect symbolism for how she felt in that moment. She smirked up at him, but her smile faded at the intensity in his gaze, the vulnerability. Did he still doubt that she wanted him?

"I want this," she said, her own voice husky with need and desire. "I want you. Never doubt that. Snow or Krampus, I don't care. I want *you*."

A tremor sort of shook him, his mouth dropping open and his eyes widening. He snapped his mouth shut, and a bright red glow sparked deep in his eyes. This time, she was sure of it. It was almost too bright to look at, but she held his gaze as she reached for his shirt. Again, he grasped her hands. This time, he held them in front of his chest for a moment, right above his heart. Slowly, he bent down and kissed her, all the passion from earlier lurking beneath the tenderness of the kiss, waiting to be released.

His hands moved to her hips, freeing her to wrap her arms around his shoulders and pull herself up as high as she could. Their height difference was presenting intriguing challenges. He must be almost two feet taller than she was. He dusted his thumbs across her stomach, then slid one hand to the zipper on her skirt, opening it, then unfastening the clasp at her waist.

Turning her so her back was to the couch, he hooked his fingers in both her skirt and her tights, tugging them down as he knelt before her again. He gently lowered her to the couch, then finished removing them, letting them drop to the floor. She was left in a scant strip of lace with the same snowflake and heart design, the fabric the softest and most delicate she'd ever seen, let alone worn.

Snow gave a rumbling growl of approval, his eyes glowing brighter as he ran his hands possessively over her thighs. When he reached her knees, he lifted them to his shoulders, leaning over her to press hot kisses against her stomach. Her core pulsed, aching to be filled by him. His mouth roved lower, his shoulders lifting her to him so that he could press his lips to her core.

Even through the fabric of her panties, she felt every breath, every flick of his tongue. Threads of pleasure wound deeper through her as he swirled his thumb against her clit, his mouth pressing harder on her core. The throbbing ache paused for a moment, then exploded through her body, lighting up her nerves. Her back arched up off the couch, her thighs clenching the sides of his head as he kept stimulating her.

When she came back down from the height of ecstasy he'd raised her to, she saw him staring up at her with those glowing red eyes, his brow lowered with a hungry look. She wanted nothing more than for him to pull her down onto his lap, her legs spread so she could straddle him and take him into her immediately. But he was still wearing all of this clothes.

Panting, she reached for his shirt and started to undo more buttons. Even with the pleasure he'd given her, she was starving for him. She wanted more. Everything he had to give. She pressed her lips to his, kissing him with more passion than she'd felt for anyone. The buttons wouldn't give, so she grabbed the fabric and pulled, trying to tear it open.

Snow chuckled against her lips, then clasped her hands and pulled them away. This time, she was the one who growled. He moved back and stood, his gorgeous body outlined by the fire behind him. She remained kneeling in front of him, watching as he opened his shirt, then pulled it loose from his pants. His abs were perfectly defined, his chest sculpted perfection. She reached out and traced the outline of his muscles, her nails scraping across his skin. Patience was something she had always prided herself on, but she had none with him. All she had was hunger.

She undid his belt and the fastener for his pants, then unzipped them and pulled them and his boxer-briefs partway down his hips, freeing his enormous erection. Crap, how was she going to manage that? She didn't even know if she could wrap her lips around it. Instead, she grasped him in both hands, her fingers not reaching around his girth.

Her core was already aching again, residual echoes of the first climax he'd given her making every nerve alive and calling out for him. He gasped as she squeezed him, giving his shaft a long, hard stroke. She couldn't resist tasting him, and brought her lips to his crown, taking as much as she could into her mouth. He let out a guttural moan that almost undid her. She stroked him faster, swirling her tongue over his sensitive flesh, imagining him buried deep inside her and timing her movements to the movements in her fantasy. He buried his fingers in her hair, groaning as he thrust against her mouth.

If this felt so fantastic, what would it actually be like to take him in her body? To feel this massive cock buried deep in her core? The thought alone almost set her off again. But this was about him. They would have time to explore each other later.

A pulse was building deep in his shaft. She increased the pressure of her hands and mouth, the speed of her strokes, building him toward his own ecstasy. His entire body shivered like the vibration of a guitar string when plucked, then he threw his head back and roared, his cock exploding into her mouth.

His hands fisted in her hair, riding her movements instead of controlling them. She matched his rhythms, taking him as high as she could, taking everything he was giving her. When he was spent, she released him and stared up into those glowing red eyes. Somehow, him being half-undressed made the view even more erotic. She couldn't wait till he was ready for more. She could do this with him forever.

Her heart seemed to stutter for a moment as she realized that was exactly what she wanted with him. Forever. She was certain he wanted the same. She would do everything in her power to prove it to him.

Chapter Nine

That had been the most intense experience of his incredibly long life. Snow stared down at Spring, his fingers still tangled in her hair, and wondered how he could ever return to a life without her.

He couldn't. It was that simple. This was his eternity staring back at him. His woman.

He released her hair, but only so he could shrug out of his shirt and cast it aside. He took her hands and pulled her to her feet, then kicked out of his shoes and quickly rid himself of his pants and undergarments and socks. She opened her lips to say something, but he had other ideas for what their mouths should be doing. He grabbed her waist and pulled her close, planting a searing, claiming kiss on her lips.

Reaching up, he lifted her breasts, flicking his thumbs over her taut nipples in the way that had made her writhe with pleasure earlier. She gasped against his mouth, spurring him on. He undid the front clasp on her bra and guided it down her arms, tossing it aside, then lowered his lips to her breasts again, giving each loving attention with his hands and mouth.

Every gasp and whimper from Spring went straight to his cock. It was already stirring again, but he knew she would need more to prepare her body for him. He might not have firsthand experience, but he had read hundreds of romances over the years of his long existence, letting himself explore this aspect of love through others' stories. So far, everything he'd learned was really paying off.

He dropped to his knees again, hands gliding over her sides, raining kisses across her stomach. He hooked his fingers in the waistband of her panties and slid them down her legs, letting them drop to the floor. The tawny curls at the apex of her legs were so close. He couldn't wait to taste her.

He lifted one of her legs and hooked it over his shoulder, holding her up with his other arm as he knelt beneath her. She gasped, her fingers digging into his shoulders as he pressed his lips to her most sensitive flesh. Still helping her to balance with one arm, he brought his free hand to her core, stroking her slit to gather her wetness.

She groaned when he slid one finger deep into her tight channel, then another, stretching her so that she would be ready for him. His cock ached, begging to take over, but he would never do anything that made her uncomfortable. He only wanted her to experience pleasure from him. Pleasure that would bind her to him forever.

He moved his hand faster, his tongue swirling on her clit. Her body stiffened, then shuddered, as she threw her head back and screamed his name. He kept going, pulling every ounce of ecstasy from her body that he could. When her hands began to relax on his shoulders, the last of his patience vanished. He had to feel her, to be inside of her.

He moved his hand away, grabbing her hips and leaning back as he pulled her down his chest. Her breasts caressed his heated skin, but his focus was elsewhere. Moving her hips, he aligned her core's entrance with his cock and pressed harder, the velvet-soft skin of her sex wrapping around him. Heat flooded him, strong enough to make his skin burn. His heart pounded frantically and his breath came in quick, panting gasps. Every part of him wanted to rise up and slam into her, but he had to go slowly, to read her reactions to make sure he didn't hurt her.

Spring groaned as he parted more of her flesh, just the tip of him inside her. She gripped his shoulders, her hips tightening against his as she spread her legs wider, pushing him deeper into her core. She gasped and paused, but then her eyes clenched tight and a pulsing beat around his crown let him know she was climaxing yet again. He dared to push his hips up, driving himself deeper.

She moved above him, arms tight around his shoulders, hips gyrating as she pulled herself up along his length, then crashed down onto it. He rose to meet her, landing deeper with every thrust. More heat coursed through him, his body alive in ways he'd never felt before. Molten pleasure arced along his nerves, spreading out from where they were joined and reaching every inch of him. He knew he wouldn't last much longer, but wanted to hold on to this moment.

He swung her around, pressing her into the faux fur rug as he spread his body on top of her. She wrapped her legs around his thighs, drawing him in deeper as he thrust into her again and again, finally burying himself to the hilt in her heat. She raked her nails down his back, hard enough to sting, a new stimulation that sent him closer to the edge of his own ecstasy. Her hands reached his backside, and she clutched it, as if spurring him on to land harder, to thrust faster. He gladly obeyed.

The heat that spread out from where they were joined grew more intense, melting his self-control as pleasure became his entire reality. Again, her back arched, head writhing against the rug as her core pulsed around him. This time, he didn't have the strength to resist. He pounded into her, her welcoming depths tightening, her slick skin pulling on his shaft. Lightning tore across his nerves, through his muscles, into his bones—the pleasure so intense, the edges of his vision dimmed. He roared as he spilled into her, filling her with his seed.

Slowly, the pleasure abated, but he couldn't bring himself to draw away. He held her tighter, letting the unity of what they had done ring through his body, mind, and soul. She was his. He would never, ever let her go.

She sighed, her body relaxing beneath him. Staring up at him with heavy-lidded eyes, she drew her hands up along his back, sending waves of goosebumps over his skin. The smile she cast up at him warmed him even more than what they had just done.

"Does time move differently in this pocket of Faerie, like in the stories?" she asked. "Because I could do this for eternity."

"We aren't in Faerie." Snow chuckled, then bent to press a kiss to the nape of her neck. "This is Aidan and Sylvia's cabin, a little ways outside town."

"Aw." Spring's lower lip plumped in a pout. "I really want to see what Faerie is like. But I'm impressed we were able to do all that in the mortal realm, because that was pure magic."

Snow laughed again, finally pulling away from her, but only so he could roll her toward the fire and wrap himself around her. She pressed her face against his chest, one arm draped over his stomach.

"It was magic for me, too," he said.

"Can you tell me about it at least? Your home?"

His heart gave a tug that she was asking about his realm. There was warmth in her question along with an understandable curiosity.

"The sky is always midnight dark, but filled with a

glowing green aurora."

"Like the aurora borealis?" she asked.

"But brighter," he said. "And it fills the entire sky. There's always a thick layer of snow on everything, and it catches the light and glows brightly enough to see by."

"I heard you and North talking about how there's never spring."

"Yeah." He held her tighter.

"But there used to be?"

"We aren't sure what happened. Even though we're ruled by the Winter Queen, there used to be seasons. One day, they just stopped. Shortly after, she came to North and me and offered us a deal."

"What kind of deal?"

"Power. The ability to change forms. Places of honor in her court as her Fairy Lords."

"Wow." Spring was quiet for a while, no doubt thinking about all he'd said.

That none of this had freaked her out was a testament to her strength of mind and will. He had never met anyone like her before, in any of the realms, Faerie or otherwise.

"You're taking this all really well, you know," he said.

"You were a lot to manage, but you did a great job warming me up." She grinned at him and waggled her eyebrows.

A laugh burst out of him, deep and loud and long. He didn't think he'd ever laughed like that before in his life.

He hugged her closer as it subsided, and she tightened her own grasp of him as well.

"You know that's not what I meant," he said.

She shrugged, an odd, far-off look entering her eyes. The crackling of the wood in the fireplace was the only sound for several minutes. He wanted to know what was going through her mind, but wouldn't press her. She would share with him when she was ready. Something in her look made him feel she was delving into a topic of great importance.

"It's all about priorities." She lifted her arm and started tracing the lines of his stomach, outlining each abdominal. "Who doesn't want to believe in fairies and magic? What I've experienced with you has been incredible—especially the most recent activities."

He chuckled lightly. He definitely agreed. The closeness they had shared had been the most amazing experience of his life. A greater magic than anything he'd encountered.

"It could have been terrifying, too," she said.

He sucked in a breath without meaning to and held it. The idea of her being afraid of him… Well, it terrified *him*. The Krampus. He hadn't realized just how much power this woman had over him until now. But he trusted her. He knew she had a good heart. One of the best he'd ever encountered. She proved it as she went on.

"But when I looked past all that, at what you're using

your power for, it stops being about dreams and becomes about reality." She raised herself on one elbow, bringing her hand to his cheek. "You help children. Children with no one in their lives who notices or cares enough to reach out to them. You give them a home and you love them. I could hear it in your voice when you shared that story about Malachi. I see it in your face every time you talk about them."

His eyes burned and the light from the fire glimmered oddly as they filled with moisture. He grasped her hand and pressed it against his cheek, closing his eyes briefly before pressing her hand to his lips for a kiss. He didn't trust his voice to speak, so he nodded, hoping his face was conveying all the love he felt for her in that moment.

"I want to learn more about your operations," she said. "You can't just whisk children off to some Faerie realm, even if it's to help them. And your home, while it sounds beautiful, it also seems... cold. Stark. Children need love more than anything, and I'm so glad you're giving them that. But they also need sunlight and trees and grass."

"I don't know how to give them those things," he said. "The Winter Queen is the one who wields that power. She's also the one who insists we bring her a child each year at Christmas."

"Hmm..." Spring's eyebrows drew together, her eyes were getting that far-off look again that he now realized meant she was thinking. She dropped her head back to his chest, one hand playing with his stomach again.

Snow waited as long as he could stand it, then prompted, "What?"

"That's weird timing, don't you think? I mean, why Christmas? Why not the Winter Solstice or really any other day of the year?"

"I never really thought about it. Maybe it's because that day centers around children already?"

"I don't know." She was quiet for a moment, then said, "I never dreamed I'd ask this question seriously, but with all these Christmas fairies being real, is Santa real, too?"

Snow chuckled and nuzzled the top of her head. "Yeah. But we call him Lord Kringle."

"Wow. I need to process that. Give me a minute."

He ran his hands down her back, enjoying the soft texture of her skin. When he looked at her again, she still had that concentrated focus in her eyes.

"Lord Kringle…" she said. "So, he's a Fairy Lord, too? Like you and the Yule Cat."

"It's me and the White Stag, now."

A pang of loss thrummed through his heart, but not as intense as it had been. North was happy living in the mortal realm and simply being the Yule Cat. And from everything Malachi had shared, Aidan and Sylvia were doing a great job taking on the roles of Lord and Lady of the North Wind.

"Okay, but what about Santa?" Spring said. "Is he part

of the Winter Queen's court as well?"

"No. She kind of has a tendency to banish people if they upset her."

"She banished *Santa*? Harsh."

"He at least gets to remain in the Yuletide Kingdom. He has a spot of land in the far reaches where he has his workshop and helpers."

Her lips pressed together as she tried to suppress a smile and failed. "Oh my God, I can't believe that's real. You have to take me there."

His own smile faltered. "As much as I hate to disappoint you, the Winter Queen decreed no one is allowed to visit him. I'm already on the Winter Queen's shit list. If I did that, my 'time-out' in the mortal realm would surely become permanent."

"That's awful." Spring rose up on her elbows again. "How could Santa have made her mad enough to get himself exiled? I mean, he's *Santa*."

"It was before my time. He was exiled right when North and I were brought into her court. I've actually never seen them in the same room together."

Snow hadn't given this much thought before, but now that Spring had pointed it out, it was hard not to think about. The Winter Queen had banished Kringle from her court, but not her kingdom. Was she supporting him in continuing his practice of bringing joy and cheer to children on Christmas? Staying in the kingdom would give him access to his people, as well as the tools and magic he needed to get his work done.

Knowing the Queen, Snow could absolutely believe she would want to keep that going. He also knew her temper. He was surprised she hadn't reassigned those duties to someone else. Something was going on there. He would have to look into it—very carefully—when she summoned him back to the Yuletide Kingdom.

Chapter Ten

Spring couldn't stop thinking about the Winter Queen and Santa. Well, she especially couldn't stop thinking about Santa. Why was it so hard to believe he was real when she'd fallen in love with the Krampus? And she *had* fallen for him. It was happening fast, but she couldn't deny the intensity of what she felt. It wasn't infatuation or wanting to be part of his magical world. She wanted *him*. She hugged him harder, pressing her face against his chest.

There had to be a reason for the Winter Queen's actions. As mercurial as fairies were said to be in all the legends, Spring had to believe that. Otherwise, how could she help keep Snow from meeting a similar fate? It would crush him to be cut off from his people—his kids. She would do everything in her power to prevent that.

"Why did the Winter Queen banish North?" Spring asked.

"He chose to be with Melanie. He loves being in the mortal realm."

"So? Haven't you guys ever heard of a timeshare?"

Snow chuckled, the rumbling sound vibrating beneath

her and warming her heart. Jack Frost had pulled her from Melanie and North's apartment. If that was all it took to go from one realm to another, what would have been the problem with North living in both worlds? Would Snow be able to? Would he even want to?

She didn't like the idea of leaving her life behind. She had worked hard to build up her business, and there were so many people who counted on her in the mortal realm. Though she didn't directly provide homes for kids, there were still a lot of organizations that benefited from her donations and pro bono efforts. She knew she was probably getting ahead of herself, but she at least wanted to know what her options were going forward.

"Is it hard to travel back and forth from the mortal realm and the Yuletide Kingdom?" she asked.

"Not at all. The first thing I taught Aidan and Sylvia was how to create a portal to take them anywhere they wanted."

"Like Frost did to us?"

"No, what he did was different. A portal is like a doorway between worlds that you can step through. He created a temporary pocket of Faerie around us."

"But he was able to move us. I mean, he dropped us in this cabin when he was done messing with us."

Snow snorted. "Frost will never be done messing with us."

"Then why did he leave us in this awesome cabin?"

Snow's chest grew as he sucked in a huge breath, his entire body tensing. She sat up to see what was bothering him. His eyes were wide and gleamed red. He launched himself from the floor and sprinted down the hall toward the door. A blast of cold air hit her as he opened it. Spring grabbed a blanket and wrapped it around herself as she followed him.

Snow stood in front of the door, silhouetted against a midnight sky filled with glowing green aurora. He had said this cabin was just outside of town. They were nowhere near far enough north to be seeing the aurora borealis. But that meant...

"That bastard," he murmured. "That unbelievable bastard. He left us in the Yuletide Kingdom."

"He recreated the whole cabin?"

"It was the only way he could get me to use my powers. I made a shield around it. The Winter Queen is sure to have detected it."

"But then—"

"She'll exile me."

"No." Spring took a few steps forward, though the chill from the door was already making her teeth chatter. "We're not going to let that happen. What can we do?"

Snow closed the door and marched down the hall, leaving a trail of snowflakes that swept across the floor as if they had a life of their own. They caught up with him, a whirlwind of snow surrounding his body and coating it in a gorgeous white uniform. The jacket had two rows of gold buttons that ran along a diagonal over his massive chest and the high collar that circled his neck was trimmed in bright red that matched the glow of his eyes. His white pants hugged his muscular legs and ended just above his gleaming black boots.

She had never seen anyone so gorgeous. Her heart raced as he strode confidently toward her, her very own fairytale prince. If she wasn't so cold, she would toss away her blanket and throw herself at him. That and the grim determination on his face held her back. He swept a hand toward her as he approached, and snowflakes flew across the floorboard, swirling up her body into the same golden dress as before. The moment the jewelry was in place, her chill vanished, along with the snow.

"His trail isn't too cold for me to track him," Snow said. "You'll be safe here till I get back."

"You're going after him? Now?"

"Without him, there's no way I can convince the Winter Queen that returning against her wishes wasn't my doing. I have to find Jack Frost."

Spring hated the thought of being trapped in a Faerie realm by herself. What if something happened to him? She tried to shake away the fear, but it must have come across in her expression.

"Don't worry." He pulled her close, leaning in to plant a searing kiss on her lips. When he finally released her, she was breathless and the room was spinning. "Nothing will ever keep me from you."

She didn't trust her voice to speak, but she nodded and forced a smile. He bent down to kiss her forehead and her heart fluttered at the sweetness of it. Then he turned and was gone, the door closing behind him and leaving her alone. She stood there for several moments, praying to anyone who was listening that Snow would be safe.

She should have been more specific.

"I thought he would never leave," a smarmy voice said right behind her.

She wheeled around to see Jack Frost standing so close, the skirts of her dress brushed against him as she turned. She backed away, and he followed, till her back was pressed against the island that separated the kitchen from the rest of the great room and she had nowhere left to escape to. Frost put one hand on the counter, leaning in close as he looked her up and down.

"You look amazing," he said. "But then, Lord Snow does have a knack for fashion. Appearances are really important to him, after being stuck as the Krampus for so long." He mock-shivered, then smiled.

"How did you get in here?"

"I built the place with my magic. Did you really think I didn't put in a back door?"

She lifted her chin and said, "What do you want?"

"Me?" He pressed his fingers to his chest, eyebrows

raised in an exaggerated expression of curiosity and innocence. "I just want you and Snow to have your very own 'Happily Ever After.'"

She snorted. She couldn't help it.

Frost tutted and shook his head. "That's not very ladylike. You'll need better manners when you meet the Winter Queen. She's big on all that formal stuff." He waved his hand dismissively. "You'll learn."

"I don't believe you."

"About the Winter Queen? No, no. She really is a stickler for that kind of thing. Just ask North's girlfriend, Melanie. She got them both banished for 'speaking impudently.'" He leaned closer and said, "Honestly, I think it was a bad call. Modern mortal women aren't afraid to state their opinions. Good for you. Just be aware that there are consequences for that when dealing with Fae royalty."

"What…" She made an exasperated sound. Every instinct was telling her that this guy didn't have a sincere bone in his body, but what he said made a lot of sense when she lined it up with all that Snow had taught her. "What's your angle? Because there's no way that you're sharing all this out of the goodness of your heart."

"Didn't you know?" Frost said, that smarmy smirk on his face that she wanted to just smack right off of him. He leaned closer and whispered, "I'm working with Santa." He rolled his eyes and spoke more conversationally. "Lord Kringle, as some call him. I'm like one of his little helpers

—temporarily."

"Why the heck would Santa want Snow and me to be a couple?" Spring asked. That didn't make any sense.

"Come on. Old Saint Nick? Bringer of joy and merriment to children of all ages? He wants everyone to be happy. Especially his family, and that includes every member of the Yuletide Court."

She folded her arms over her chest and glared at him. "A court that you would have been a Lord in, if it wasn't for Snow."

Frost made a dismissive snort and rolled his eyes again. "Like I'd want to be a Fairy Lord. At the beck and call of the Winter Queen? Have her bossing me around all the time?" He waved his hand as if shooing something away. "Not my scene."

"Then why have you been harassing us?" Spring said, exasperation lacing her voice.

"Harassing you?" He laughed. "You have it all wrong. I've been matchmaking."

"What?" Her mind spun. What was he talking about?

"I knew that Snow would never spend time with a mortal unless he thought he had something to make up for. He's such an honorable guy." Frost somehow managed to make even his compliments sound condescendingly derogatory.

"That little accident that brought you two together?" he went on. "Him slipping on the ice, right as you were looking out the window to see him fall? And then the bus coming, and yet another patch of ice making you land on top of him as you tried to pull him back?"

Frost made a tutting sound. "I hate to tell you, princess, but that meet cute was all me. I arranged it, just like I made sure you were aware of his true nature, both as a Fairy Lord and as the Krampus. Figured it'd be best to get all that drama out in the open and over with as soon as possible so you two could get on with... bonding." He waggled his eyebrows suggestively.

Spring's cheeks prickled, her eyes wide with disbelief. She hated feeling like she had been manipulated into this, even if it had resulted in her and Snow being together. And if she felt this enraged, how would it affect Snow? His feelings for her?

"Do you know what you've done?" Spring snapped.

Frost's lips pulled into a downturned line at her tone, but he waved his hand in a circle as if to encourage her to speak. "Enlighten me."

"You've ruined any chance we had at real happiness. There will always be that sliver of doubt now. Is it really love? Or is it just another spell?"

"My magic doesn't work that way," Frost said. "I'm not Cupid. I just... created certain situations that might lead to entertaining results and sat back to enjoy the fun. I had no idea it would end up this good—that was all Kringle. But, after all is said and done, you're perfect for each other, I assure you."

"I know that," she bit out each word. "He is everything I ever dreamed of and more. He's the one who's going to wonder for the rest of time if he really loves me or if this is just another fairy asshole trying to control him."

"I can explain it to him if you'd like," Frost said with a beatific smile.

She jerked forward, jabbing her finger into his chest so that *he* was the one who backed away. "You will stay the hell away from my man, or I swear to whatever gods are real I will build the biggest barbecue pit in history and roast you over it on a spit until all that's left of you is steam."

Deep laughter washed over her. She turned to see Snow standing behind her in the doorway, his arms loose at his sides and a huge smile on his face. He shook his head as he quieted.

"Woman," he said. "After hearing you say that, I will never, ever doubt that you are my perfect match."

Chapter Eleven

"What are you doing back so soon?" Frost asked, his brow furrowing.

Snow chuckled, glad to see the asshole genuinely perplexed. "You think I couldn't detect a fake trail? I knew you had doubled back within two minutes. I didn't know you were stupid enough to harass my woman, though." He walked up next to Spring and wrapped an arm around her, tucking her against his side.

"Harass?" Frost took a step farther away from them. "No. Spring and I were just getting to know each other better."

"Yes," Spring said, her voice oozing saccharine sweetness. "And Frost here knows me well enough now to be aware that I will rip out his spleen if he doesn't tell the Winter Queen that he is the one who transported us here—without our knowledge or permission."

Snow let out a rumbling growl of approval. He knew that Spring was strong. He hadn't known how fierce she was until he returned and heard her lighting into Frost. Sure, she didn't have a chance of really doing anything to him. Frost was a powerful Fae in his own right. But Snow had a feeling that wouldn't matter to Spring. She would stand up to anyone that she thought meant him harm.

His chest filled with warmth at the thought. No one had ever stood up for him before. Not like this. He reached down and trailed a finger along her jaw, lifting her face to his, then bent down and kissed her. He pushed all his love and passion into that tender kiss, willing her to understand the words he hadn't had a chance to say yet.

"You're welcome," Frost said, cutting into their moment.

They both turned to him, scowling.

"I don't remember thanking you," Spring said.

"And I forgive you for your terrible manners." Frost bowed lightly.

"Fairies don't normally thank each other," Snow said, addressing Spring. "It can be seen as acknowledging a debt. There's always an angle." He focused on Frost and said, "We owe you nothing, Frost."

Frost tutted, shaking his head. "So ungrateful."

"What is it that you want?" Spring said. "Power? A favor?"

"I don't want power." Frost rolled his eyes. "I want freedom. Power is only a means to an end."

"What do you want freedom from?" Snow asked. "Are you looking to change courts? Because they're all pretty much the same."

"Exactly," Frost snapped. For a moment, a look of

anger crossed his features. It was the most genuine expression Snow had ever seen from the Fae. It didn't last long

"You got me." Frost smiled and lifted both arms as if surrendering. "I don't want to be claimed by any court."

"Every Fae is claimed," Snow said.

"And what kind of shitty system is that?" Frost paced back and forth in the small space between the kitchen island and the couch. "Claimed as subjects by the most powerful Fae around, but what they really mean is that we're resources at their beck and call. Little chess pieces to be moved around the board and used however they please." He paused near Spring, arms crossed over his chest. In a calmer voice, he said, "It's really not all that bad. Welcome to the family," and smirked.

"Wow, you've really sold me on it," Spring said. "But if you want me to be excited about Team Yuletide Fae, maybe do us a solid and confess to the Winter Queen that you're the reason Snow is here against her wishes so that he doesn't get permanently exiled."

"Mmm, can't do that," Frost said.

Spring let out a frustrated grunt. "Why not?"

"Couples grow stronger when they go through adversity together," Frost said. "Besides, you're not the only pair I'm trying to help."

"What?" Spring's voice rose, an exasperated edge to it.

Snow expected nothing else from Frost. He was

actually surprised the Fae had been so forthcoming. But who was the other couple he was trying to help? North and Melanie, maybe? Was he trying to get the Winter Queen to lift her banishment of North so that he could visit his home? Snow had to admit to himself that he would love that. At the moment, he was most concerned with avoiding the same fate.

"The Winter Queen will banish me when she finds me here," Snow said. "I'm surprised she hasn't shown up already."

"Well, you did that whole shielding thing." Frost leaned a bit closer. "Very impressive, I must admit. It did, however use a bunch of your magic, so as soon as the shield drops, she'll sense your mark all over this spot."

"Then he can just keep the shield up," Spring said. "Can you do that?"

"It'll be a strain on my power, but I think so." Snow nodded.

"See?" Frost said. "You're already problem solving together. You two are going to stand the test of time. I'm sure of it."

"Your faith in us warms my heart." Spring packed an impressive amount of sarcasm in her tone. Frost only laughed.

"I still don't understand why you're doing this," Snow said. "How is this going to free you from the Court of the Yuletide Fae? Whose favor are you trying to earn?"

"Come on," Frost said. "You said yourself that we're going to be claimed by someone, no matter what we do. Whoever has the most power gets to boss everyone else around. I just need someone who understands that I want to be left to my own devices. I have my own projects, you know."

The thought was not comforting. What kind of projects would Jack Frost be up to?

"I am starting to think I have a bit of a knack for this matchmaking thing, though," Frost said. "I might be able to give Cupid a run for his money."

"Wait, Cupid is real?" Spring asked. Snow and Frost both turned to her, each arching an eyebrow. She nodded. "Right. I have a lot to learn, apparently."

"And soon you'll have all the time in eternity to learn it," Frost said.

Spring's eyes narrowed. "What do you mean by that?"

Snow already knew. They hadn't had a chance to broach the subject yet, but Snow had begun to think of ways to bring Spring into the Yuletide Kingdom and what that would mean for them both. He was immortal. He couldn't stand the thought of forever without her.

"He means that for us to be together, you'd have to become like me," Snow said.

"Like *us*," Frost corrected. "You need to become a fairy."

Frost linked his thumbs together and spread his hands,

waggling his fingers like wings in an approximation of a butterfly. Snow just rolled his eyes at Frost, then turned to Spring and ran his hands along her arms. His chest felt tight, nerves churning his stomach. This was not how or when he wanted to have this conversation, but there was no way around it.

"I know this is all happening fast, but if you truly want to be with me—" he began.

"I do," Spring said. "Of course, I do."

Frost leaned behind her so that Snow could see his face but she couldn't. He mouthed, 'of course,' silently.

"Do you mind?" Snow said.

"Me?" Frost pressed his fingers to his chest. "Not at all. Continue."

Snow let out an exasperated breath and shook his head. He would deal with Frost in a minute.

Snow turned back to Spring and said, "I want to be with you, too. Not just for your mortal lifetime. Forever."

She smiled, her eyes lighting up as she nodded. "That sounds wonderful."

"Even if you have to deal with assholes like him?" Snow nodded his head toward Frost.

"I think I can handle it," she said.

"I can hear you, you know," Frost said.

Spring ignored him. "Is that something you can do?"

Snow had been expecting this question from her, and dreading it. He was powerful, but he couldn't grant immortality to others, effectively making them Fae. Very few had that ability. If the Winter Queen didn't accept Spring, he would have to petition someone else. The political ramifications of asking a ruler of another Court of the Fae were too horrible for him to contemplate, but that only left him with Lord Kringle. Kringle had been the one to make Melanie immortal. Maybe he could do it again for Spring. But Snow asking him would not sit well with the Winter Queen. Snow and Spring might have to join North and Melanie in exile.

"It isn't," Snow said. "But we can find someone who can."

Spring narrowed her eyes as she scrutinized him. "What aren't you telling me?"

"Just…" He tried to find a way to explain that wouldn't burden her, yet wouldn't keep her from the truth. "It's going to be very tricky to navigate. But I'm sure we can figure it out."

She smiled at him and wrapped her arms around his waist. "I am, too."

"See?" Frost said. "Look at you. Facing obstacles together."

"Are you still here?" Spring said, glaring at him.

"I am." Frost cocked his head to the side, lips pressed in a thoughtful line. "But it's about time I left." He took a few steps back and pressed his hand to his chest. "For what it's worth, I believe in you two. You will absolutely get through this and be stronger for it."

"Wait, get through what?" Snow said, taking a step closer.

Frost smiled, then snapped his fingers. In a puff of vapor, he vanished.

So did the cabin—and with it, the sphere of obscuring power Snow had linked to it.

Snow's eyes grew wide as he saw nothing but a forest clearing around them. The aurora overhead reflected off the snow coating the ground and the branches of the trees, giving them plenty of light to see by. Behind him, he felt a crackle of raw power so intense, he knew what that light would reveal. He turned in a slow circle, till he was facing the Winter Queen.

Chapter Twelve

Where the heck had the cabin gone? One minute, Spring was snuggled up next to Snow, standing in front of a warm fire, the next, they were in the middle of a clearing in a forest of evergreens and denuded trees. Everything was cast in a gold-green glow from the aurora above, the trees' branches nothing more than dark shadows to her vision. Snow stiffened beside her and sucked in a breath. He held it as they both spun around to see what was behind them. Or rather, who.

A tall woman stood a few paces away, her hands clasped elegantly in front of herself. Her blonde hair was pulled back in a tight chignon that was held in place partly by a crown of platinum spikes, like a starburst around her head. Diamonds glittered in the light both from above and that she seemed to radiate herself. Her skin was as white as the snow she stood upon, and her dress a pale blue silk, like moonlight wrapped around her. Her high cheekbones and pointed chin and nose might have made her more beautiful, except for the harsh frown of her red lips and the pinched skin around her emerald-green eyes. This had to be the Winter Queen.

Spring swallowed hard. The air was thick with tension. Snow had yet to release that breath he had taken. He stared at the woman with wide eyes, his mouth hanging open.

"My Lord Snow," the Winter Queen said.

Spring tried not to be irked by the claim in her greeting. She might have made it, if Snow hadn't immediately dropped to one knee, his head bowed.

"Majesty," Snow said.

Spring didn't know what to do. She sort of curtseyed briefly, but mostly wanted to draw as little attention to herself as possible. That didn't work out, either.

"Another mortal woman?" the Winter Queen said. "Why have you brought her here?"

"He didn't bring me," Spring quickly said. "Jack Frost did. He brought both of us and—"

"Spring." Snow reached out and grasped her hand. She looked down at him and he shook his head. The skin at the corners of his eyes was pinched with worry.

"Jack Frost has been wronged enough," the Winter Queen said. "Do not dare attempt to cast blame on the one who should have been Lord of the North Wind."

Snow bowed his head lower. Spring couldn't stand seeing him like this. Sure, the Winter Queen was his... liege or something, but that didn't mean he should have to grovel around her. What kind of person was she?

She's not a person, Spring reminded herself. *She's a fairy.*

But Snow was kind. So was North, from everything Spring had seen. Maybe they were the exceptions instead of the rules? Jack Frost had certainly been a dick.

"You defy me yet again," the Winter Queen said. "Returning to my kingdom without my leave."

"But—" Spring stopped herself as Snow squeezed her hand tighter.

"You were always my most loyal subject," the Winter Queen said.

'Were?' As in past-tense? Was Snow about to be exiled?

"Majesty, I remain loyal." Snow's voice was tight with strain.

"Perhaps." The Winter Queen was silent for a few moments, then said, "Perhaps I will give you a chance to prove that to me. You shall perform penance."

Snow bowed deeper again. "As you decree."

"But he didn't do anything wrong," Spring burst out. It was just too much. She couldn't stand watching Snow being treated this way. "You can't just—"

The Winter Queen spoke over Spring, voice rising. "You may begin your penance *after* you return this woman to the mortal realm. Spin a charm to take her memory of this place, the Fae, and of you."

"What?" Spring nearly shouted.

At the same time, Snow sprang to his feet at last. "Majesty, I beg you—"

"Beg?" The Winter Queen snapped. "You, the Krampus, resort to begging? What has this woman done to you?"

Snow looked at Spring, his expression filled with wonder. "She's opened my eyes, my mind, my heart to a love I never dreamed I would experience."

"She has weakened you," the Queen said.

Snow shook his head. "She's made me stronger."

"I will not have her in my kingdom," the Queen said.

"Then I'll live in the mortal realm and he can visit me there," Spring said.

"Spring…" Snow's voice trailed off.

"I forbid it!" The Winter Queen slashed her hand through the air. Above, the aurora shivered, its green glow cutting out for a moment and throwing them into darkness. The branches shook from a chill wind that swirled around her, then vanished.

How far did Spring dare push this? She looked up at Snow, at the turmoil in his features, and knew she would do anything for him.

She turned back to the Queen and said, "We can find a way to make this work."

"He must prove his loyalty to me and no other," the Queen said. "One world or another. That is his choice."

No…

"Please, all his children are here." Spring couldn't be responsible for Snow being exiled. She knew how that would hurt him. "His family needs him."

"Indeed," the Queen said. "Which is why you must not distract him from his duties. Your paths are different. You must let him go."

"But I can help him, help all of you." Spring dared to take a step closer to the Winter Queen, her voice pleading "Please, haven't you ever been in love?"

The Winter Queen's brow drew down over her eyes, her voice rising as she spoke. "I know all I need of mortal love—fickle and weak. As impermanent as your insignificant lives."

Wait... She was in love with a mortal. Maybe she still is...

It was obvious in the pain that flooded her features, the passion in her tone. What had happened that had hardened her heart? At the same time, she still had warmth toward children. Spring could never hate the Winter Queen, knowing how they both shared that dream of helping others. There had to be a way Spring could make her understand that one hurt—or even many—didn't mean she had to close off her heart.

Begging didn't seem likely to work with her. Plus, that wasn't Spring's style. No, she was going to push this in her own way.

"If we're so insignificant, why bother our children?" Spring demanded, crossing her arms defiantly. "They're mortal, too."

The Winter Queen drew herself up taller. "Only when we find them. Once they have joined my court, they become Fae."

"Once you adopt them," Spring said.

The Queen's mouth opened briefly, but then she snapped it shut again. Spring was definitely gaining ground.

"You bring them into your family," Spring said. "Can't you do the same with me?"

"This is what you want, then?" The Queen narrowed her eyes. "Power? Immortality?"

"No." Spring turned back to Snow and said, "I want to be with him. And I want to help people—to help children. I want to stand at Snow's side and support him. To help him in his life's work—the same work I've always dreamed of doing myself. Helping as many children as we can in the best way that we can. Working together to make a better life for them. Can't you, of all beings, understand that?"

Spring looked back at the Queen and her breath caught in her chest. The Winter Queen backed away a step, and then another. Her hand was clutched in front of her heart as if she was desperately trying to hold it in one piece. She shook her head sharply.

In a voice that was barely above a whisper, she said, "I can not."

She looked so lost and alone in that moment, that

Spring's heart felt as though it might break. Whatever had happened to her, this was the crux of it. At the same time, Snow stared at the Queen with wide eyes, his skin drawn and bloodless. He looked... afraid. Terrified, even. What frightened Spring the most was that she wasn't sure what he was afraid of.

The Queen could exile him, but they could make things work in the mortal realm, couldn't they? He had said he had ways of communicating with his people, so they wouldn't be completely cut off. Was he considering erasing Spring's memories of himself?

No. He would never do such a thing. She knew his heart, the goodness and protectiveness there. She hated that the Winter Queen was trying to give him an ultimatum. Spring still couldn't shake the feeling that there was more at stake than he was telling her.

The Winter Queen took a few steps away, shaking her head again, then said, "You have heard my decree. Choose. Are you no longer my Lord Snow?"

"Majesty..." Snow bowed his head. "There is no choice to be made. My heart belongs to Spring. Forever."

Chapter Thirteen

"You choose her over me?" The Winter Queen's voice was low and harsh. "Over your sworn duties as a Lord of the Court of the Yuletide Fae?"

"Majesty," Snow said, stepping forward.

"So be it." Her face became impassive as she stood straighter. "Then you are Lord of Endless Snow no more. You are merely as I found you. The Krampus."

"Wait—" His eyes widened in shock, his stomach flooded with icicles of dread. She couldn't truly mean to turn him back. Could she?

With a flick of her wrist that was as casual as it was cruel, he felt the power of the Lord of Endless Snow leach from his body, summoned back to her. As it left him, curving horns rose up from his head, his shoulders hunched, and claws sprang forth from his fingers. His chin and nose jutted out from his face far enough that he could see them with his own eyes, his cheekbones rising within his periphery as well. His legs morphed and sprouted fur, his feet changed to hooves. All that he had left to cover himself was the tattered remains of his jacket, though his thick fur concealed his skin.

He looked down at his hands, their skin was rough and patchy, sharp, black claws curling at their fingertips. How could he ever hold Spring again like this? How could he let her see him?

He curled away from her, intending to run, but felt her hands on his arm, holding tight.

"Don't even think of bolting," she said, her voice strong and calm. "Look at me. Snow... Look at me."

This was better. Get it over and done with. Let his hope for anything more than this bleak and lonely existence die along with her love for him. He shook his head and turned, standing straighter so that she could see his full, terrifying form.

"Not Snow," he said in a guttural growl. "The Krampus."

Her eyes widened slightly as she looked at him, but only for a moment. Then she smirked at him. That same smirk, filled with warmth and a mystery that no longer bothered him but only drew him in.

"You've always been the Krampus," she said. "I've known that from the start. But you're also Snow, Lord or not. My Snow."

She reached up and cupped his cheek, pulling him down to her. His heart thudded like the thunder of a herd of stampeding reindeer. Did she truly mean to kiss him? Even in this hideous form? She smiled at him—a true smile—just before their lips touched. Warmth flooded him, along with the same electric pleasure that always filled him when they kissed. Taking great care, he wrapped his hands around her waist, keeping his claws from prickling her clothing or scratching her skin.

She wrapped her arms around his neck and clung to him, moving to his ear to whisper, "I don't care what you look like. I know who you are within. And I love you."

"I love you, too," he said, holding her close.

He looked up at the Winter Queen to see her face a mask of disbelief. Her chest rose and fell quickly with near-panicked breaths. What little color she had had faded from her face and her eyes were wide as she stared at them.

"Very well," she said, composing herself once more. "Since you are so determined to be together, it's only fitting that you match."

The Winter Queen lifted her arms in the air, a terrible energy gathering around them. Bolts of lightning arced through clouds of snow and frost that swirled around her. She raised her hands above her head, the greatest look of fury on her face that the Krampus had ever seen.

He held Spring close, and whispered, "I'm so sorry."

"Elysa!" A loud voice rang through the air, resonating with enough power to make the Krampus stagger.

He held tighter to Spring as they helped each other keep their balance, turning to try to find the source. The Krampus froze as he saw that the fury in the Winter

Queen's face had been replaced with shock and something he couldn't name. Her cheeks flushed pink and her eyes were wide, her lips parted. The energy that had gathered around her dropped harmlessly to the ground and disappeared. She turned slowly, stepping aside to reveal Lord Kringle standing several feet away.

He looked... different. His dark red jacket was replaced with a bright red coat that buttoned on a diagonal up one side. The lapels were lined with white fur and more of the same peeked out from his cuffs. He wore a broad, shiny black belt and matching boots, with darker red pants tucked into them. The buckle on his belt was a platinum snowflake, the symbol of the Winter Queen. His white hair was combed back from his forehead and swept around his shoulders, and his beard had been neatly trimmed.

It was his eyes that were most changed, though. The mirth that usually twinkled in their blue depths was blurred by tears, and deep lines of pain shone in the wrinkles at the corners of his eyes.

"Enough, Elysa," he said, his voice no longer echoing with command. "It's me that you're mad at. Don't take it out on your boys."

"You aren't supposed to be here," she whispered in hoarse tones. "I didn't want... I didn't ever want to see you again."

"I know and I'm sorry," Kringle said. "I stayed away for as long as I could. But I miss you. I miss you terribly."

The Winter Queen drew herself up taller, clasping her shaking hands in front of her as if she was afraid she might reach for him. A day ago, Snow wouldn't have understood. Now… Now, he thought he might have a better idea of what had been going on ever since North had refused to bring the Winter Queen a tribute all those years ago.

"You abandoned me," she said, and power crackled through her words.

Snow pulled Spring closer, inching away from the pair. Kringle showed no sign of fear. Only sadness. He approached the Queen, who arched away from him, though her feet seemed rooted to the spot.

"I was stubborn and single-minded." Kringle shook his head. "I only wanted to feel joy, to focus on bringing more of that into the world. What you wanted—"

"What I wanted was to *help* those children who needed us most," she yelled. "Not simply leave them toys once a year and be done with it."

Kringle's eyes widened. His mouth opened and closed a few times, then shut as he nodded.

"We couldn't…" He paused to clear his throat. "We couldn't help all of them. We still can't."

"That shouldn't stop us from trying to help the ones we *can*," she said, her voice nearly breaking.

"You're right," Kringle said. "You've always been stronger than I. You can look at the ones left behind—the ones struggling and lashing out—and it gives you a sense of purpose. For me, it brings despair that fills my heart and paralyzes me." His eyes shimmered as his voice turned to an intense whisper. "I'm no good to anyone like that."

The Winter Queen stared at him in stunned silence, her own mouth dropping open. A line of frost flowed down her cheek from the corner of her eye, forming a tiny teardrop of ice that softly clinked as it landed on the ground.

This was what had caused them to part ways? Why she had reached out to the Krampus and the Yule Cat to help her with her cause in helping children? No wonder she had lashed out so harshly when North refused. She had already been abandoned once. Now, she thought it was happening again with Snow. But it wasn't. He had to find a way to convince her of that. To show her that they could still help with her mission, but in a better way. With even more help, especially with what Lord Kringle was saying.

"Kris…" she said.

Kringle dared to reach out and grasp her hands, pulling her closer to him.

"I never meant to abandon you," he said. "I should have faced my fears and shared them with you, not retreated to my workshop and ignored them. I should have supported you and not ignored what you wanted. We could have found a better way to overcome our differences if I only had tried harder. Been less intent on my own goals. But, maybe together, we can find a way forward now."

As he pulled her closer, he whispered, "I swear on

everything I am, I will not fail you again. Please, give me another chance to love you. Properly this time. As partners."

She smiled at him and nodded. "That is all I ever wanted." A tear flowed down her cheek, and this time, it left no trail of frost. She shook her head and said, "I could never resist you."

Lord Kringle and the Winter Queen leaned toward each other, fingers intertwined as they pressed their lips together in a tender kiss. Light spread over the horizon behind them, the aurora above retreating for the first time in Snow's memory. Crocuses burst forth through the white coating the ground, surrounding them with brilliant dots of pale or rich purple and vibrant gold. In the distance, the Krampus heard a songbird pierce the silence of the fallen snow.

Brilliant light spun around Kringle's head as a small crown of platinum and diamonds settled upon it. The light also swept over the Winter Queen, transforming her crown to one that matched his. Her nearly-colorless dress deepened to a rich emerald green that matched her eyes, her skirts became fuller, and an elegant apron appeared tied around her waist. A few wisps of hair loosened from what was now more a bun than a chignon, softening her features as she pulled back and smiled at her husband.

"You're Mrs. Claus," Spring exclaimed. "Mrs. Santa Claus!"

The Winter Queen arched an eyebrow at her. Snow bowed low, tugging on Spring's sleeve.

"Majesty," he said.

Spring grimaced, but then made a quick curtesy. He had no idea that sarcasm could be expressed so eloquently in such a brief movement. His stomach clenched, but the Winter Queen only smiled.

"I suppose I deserve that," she said. She turned to the Krampus and added, "But you don't deserve this. Rise, Lord Snow."

A chill breeze swept over him, snow and ice began wrapping around his horns and claws and disintegrated them with their passing. He felt his chin and nose shrink, along with his cheekbones, and his legs returned to what had become normal to him over the thousands of years he'd spent in this human form. He looked down, patting his body to ensure he was once more himself.

"I'm Snow again," he said, almost giddy with relief. "Not the Krampus."

Spring wrapped her arms around his waist and looked up at him, that smirk he had grown to love firmly in place and her eyes filled with love.

"You will always be the Krampus—my Krampus," she said. "And there's nothing wrong with that."

The breeze warmed, or maybe it was the love he felt for her filling him. The love she radiated right back. He leaned down and kissed her, not nearly as tender as the

Kringles' kiss had been, but filled with all his passion. He buried his hands in her hair, restating his claim, pouring his gratitude and amazement that this incredible woman had chosen him, of every being in all the realms, to claim as her own.

He pulled back to see that the ground around them had thawed, the snow was retreating as he watched. They stood in a circle of greening grass, the bare trees surrounding them were covered in buds that began to unfurl into beautiful petals and leaves popped out along their branches. Birds of vibrant blues, greens, and yellows hopped among them, along with the Redbirds that had been the only bird to be found in the land before. The sun beamed down at them from a clear blue sky.

"My dear," the Winter Queen said, approaching them. "I have behaved so poorly."

Spring shook her head. "I think I get it. You were both trying to find your way. It can be hard to find paths that intertwine, even if you're aiming for the same goal. And the Fae are... passionate and powerful beings." She smiled up at Snow, but then turned back to the Queen, her expression serious. "But listen, no more snatching kids. There's a better way to go about this."

"Oh?" The Queen's eyes widened, her eyebrows rising on her forehead.

A thread of worry wound through Snow's stomach, as he wondered how the Queen would react to being corrected by a mortal. His worry vanished as she smiled warmly.

"Please go on," the Winter Queen said. "I would love to hear your thoughts."

"Well…" Spring looked up at him and he nodded encouragement. "There are systems in place in the mortal realm. Foster care, orphanages. Places that could use more resources and support. Instead of trying to help one or two kids every year, why not send some of your people to work with them and use some of these magic diamonds and stuff to fund organizations that are making a huge difference for many?"

The Queen's eyebrows rose higher. "That is a very intriguing idea."

It was more than an intriguing idea to Snow. It was a fantastic idea. And with his holdings in the mortal realm, he could definitely make an impact. He turned to Kringle, watching the man's reactions carefully as he jumped into the conversation.

"We would have to move slowly," Snow said. "To prevent unbalancing the economic systems we'd be influencing."

"Mortal economies are not my realm." The Winter Queen laughed. She turned to Snow and Spring and said, "But I have a feeling the two of you would be well suited to make strides with this."

Spring's eyes widened and she clutched Snow's arm

tighter. "Us? Me?"

The Winter Queen stepped forward, extending her hands. This time, Spring didn't look to him for encouragement. She stepped right forward, meeting the Queen and clasping their hands together.

"My child, you have done such a great service for my kingdom." The Queen looked back at Kringle, her cheeks turning pinker, then smiled at Snow with such warmth, his heart fluttered in his chest. "For my family. I would ask more of you, though."

Spring swallowed hard enough that Snow saw her throat work, but she nodded.

"Be my agent in the mortal realm," the Queen said. "Stand by Lord Snow's side and help him—and the rest of us—navigate this new path. I can sense in your heart that you have the will, and I can see in your mind that you have the ability."

"I… I don't know what to say." Spring smiled. "Except yes."

"Then there is only one more thing we must do." The Winter Queen smiled back, nodding. "I cannot have a mortal doing my bidding. The other courts would see it as weakness, and we dare not let down our guard."

Spring nodded, her eyes wide. The Queen dropped her hands, but only to clasp Spring's face and draw her close.

"Therefore, I welcome you into the Court of the Yuletide Fae—Lady Spring." She bent forward and lightly kissed Spring's forehead.

A swirl of snow and frost rose around them, coating Spring's skin and quickly soaking into it. She glowed with a beautiful golden light, as bright as the sun, as bright as the heart full of love and caring that Snow knew beat within her breast. Flowers sprang up amidst the grass at her feet, spreading out through the clearing until it was filled with color. The buzzing drone of bees joined in with the chorus of songbirds that trilled their pleasure from the trees.

Two gleaming white deer flew through the sky, their golden antlers gleaming in the sunlight, legs moving as if they were running on the air—Aidan and Sylvia drawn by the light and warmth emanating from the clearing. They landed in the grass, gold eyes wide with wonder as they looked around the clearing, then they turned toward Spring and the Winter Queen and bowed on their front legs.

Spring's hair shone with a lustrous sheen of gold, power radiating from her unlike anything Snow had ever sensed before. The Winter Queen straightened, then pulled Spring into her arms. Kringle stepped to Snow's side.

"Lady *Spring*," Snow whispered low enough that only Kringle would hear.

"We will deal with it should the need arise." Kringle nodded to Snow, before crossing to the women and embracing them both.

Snow's chest felt overfull as he looked at the group

before him. His family. If the Court of the Springtime Fae or any other courts had a problem with Spring's title, Snow—the Krampus—would be ready to protect her. To protect all of them. Though, with the power emanating from her, he doubted that would be necessary.

Spring turned to him, her eyes glowing with the promise of their future and all the good it would hold. All the love. She ran to him, throwing her arms around his neck and pulling him to her for a long, passionate kiss. When they paused at last, he looked into the eyes of his love and said, "I guess spring isn't so bad after all."

Epilogue

Lord Kringle watched as his family gathered together around one of the huge ovens in the Yule Cat's bakery. Elysa was sharing one of her favorite recipes for Chocolate Crinkle Cookies with North and Melanie, the three chatting excitedly about different ways of enhancing the flavor. Snow and Spring had their arms around each other, laughing as Aidan snuck a pinch of raw cookie dough, only to have his hand swatted by Sylvia.

A chilly breeze tickled the back of Kringle's neck. He glanced over his shoulder, then quietly exited the kitchen into the bakery's main room. Jack Frost was lounging in North's favorite window seat, one knee pulled up, his foot on the cushion, the other dangling on the floor. He was drawing little snowmen in frost on the glass.

"Well, that all worked out rather well," Frost said.

"It did indeed. And I thank you."

"Ugh." Frost rolled his eyes. "All this time living among fairies, and you still haven't learned not to thank us."

"Mortal manners are hard to shake," Kringle said, chuckling lightly.

Frost smirked and shook his head. He rose from his seat and crossed over to stand near Kringle.

"Your um 'methods' were not exactly how I'd have gone about this," Kringle said. "Did you have to be..."

"Such a dick about it?" Frost offered.

Kringle's eyes widened and he laughed, his cheeks tingling in embarrassment. "Well, I wouldn't have used that word exactly."

"You are adorable." Frost chuckled, then put his hands on Kringle's shoulders. "And now... you owe me a favor."

A chill swept over Kringle, but he nodded. "That I do. I trust you know that I won't do anything against my nature, however."

Frost placed a hand on his own chest and shook his head. "You wound me." He stepped back, smirk firmly in place. "Now that everything is clear, I'll take my leave." He bowed low and said, "Santa." Then burst into a cloud of frost, tiny particles of ice hovering in the air for a moment before vanishing.

"Everything okay out here?" Snow walked up to Kringle's side, sniffing the air and glancing around as if searching for danger.

"Everything's fine."

Kringle patted his arm and turned him back toward the kitchen. He cast a final glance around the bakery, his eyes settling on the snowmen that Frost had drawn—two full sized, and between them... a smaller one. The trio held each other's stick hands, large, happy smiles drawn on their faces with loving detail.

Kringle's heart warmed and he nodded, thinking of Frost. There was something he could do for that boy. He just needed a bit of time to figure it out. In the meantime, his family had been reunited at last. Lord Kringle—Santa —intended to enjoy every moment of it.

—

Thank you so much for reading *The Krampus!* I didn't intend to write this trilogy, but when the ideas starting pouring forth, I knew I had to capture their magic on the page. It's been such an adventure! Thank you for journeying through the Yuletide Kingdom with me. I'm sure we'll be visiting this universe again. In the meantime, please enjoy this excerpt from a different type of universe, but one that holds the same theme of outsiders finding their place among humans with hearts full of love and warmth. "Found Family" is at the foundation of all my worlds, whether they're Paranormal, Urban Fantasy, or Science Fiction Romance.

Gray Card

The Department of Homeworld Security
Book One

Is he after her heart or her planet?

Evelyn Chambers is a nerdgirl and proud of it. When she finds out that her drop-dead gorgeous best friend is an alien general with only three days left on Earth, she has to wrap her head around too much at once. Aliens are real, and if she wants to keep hanging out with one, she'll have to marry him!

Adam Smith has never seen a planet as beautiful as Earth or a woman as enticing as Evelyn. His government wants him to re-enlist, but when Evelyn suggests marriage to help him stay, Adam realizes that what he really wants is her—and he'll sacrifice everything to be with her.

Can he convince his government—and Evelyn—that he's looking for more than a Gray card?

Chapter One

Two things were working at ruining Evelyn's day. First, she was wearing a dress to try to get Adam—the love of her life—to see her as something other than a friend. Second, Adam was having an argument with some jackass.

With irritating sweat trickling down her spine from the relentless summer heat and Adam so obviously upset, she wondered if now was the best time to try to make the leap. She watched him as she debated the wisdom of her decision.

Evelyn had never seen Adam's dark eyebrows furrowed over his perfectly straight nose. She'd never seen his gorgeous eyes—one the blue of the waters off Oahu and the other as green as the immaculate grass in the park behind him—narrowed in anger.

The skin over his jaw held its usual light coat of stubble. She could still clearly see the taut masseter muscle flexing within his cheek. Even his face was toned.

What was she thinking? Blonde-from-a-bottle, too small up top, too big at the hips, her narrow face accented by huge horn-rimmed glasses...

Wait—superheroes sometimes wore big glasses to put people off-guard and conceal their strength. She wore them to remind herself that she was strong too.

Evelyn wasn't going to let herself be cowed by her

measurements or society's standards. She was going to go for it. Eventually. As soon as she could get herself to move.

The man Adam had been talking to sauntered off, hands in the pockets of his dark suit. He would probably have a heat stroke any minute, but looked as though he hadn't a care in the world. Unlike Adam.

Adam had his hands on his hips, feet braced far apart as he stared at the sky. His muscular legs couldn't be hidden by the khaki cargo shorts he always wore and his jade green T-shirt seemed barely able to keep itself together over the joy of embracing his broad chest.

Reining in her libido, Evelyn wiped her damp palms on her dress to dry them off, then slid her glasses farther up her nose. This wasn't the time to push the envelope. She could tell him how she felt later. From the looks of it, right now Adam needed a friend. She would be that friend.

She only wished she was in her normal clothes. Jeans and one of the T-shirts she'd made for her gaming group during her undergrad studies would be much more comfortable. She'd been wearing something similar when she first met Adam, plus a sign around her neck that said, "Help! I'm an alien stranded on this primitive planet!" It was her standard costume when she went to comic book conventions.

Adam had actually been concerned when he approached her, and not because he thought she was nuts

—like most people. It didn't take long for her to figure out he wasn't local, with all the weird idiosyncrasies in his use of English. Until today, she actually had never seen him speak with anyone else aside from ordering food at a restaurant.

Time to find out how she could help.

The sidewalk baked her feet through her sandals as she approached him. "I'd ask if everything is all right, but it obviously isn't."

Adam closed his eyes and took one last deep breath. "I've had better days."

"You don't look like you're up for a bunch of personal questions, so I just have one. Do you want to talk about it?"

"Not really." He finally looked at her, apparently not registering her dress at all. "I thought we were meeting at your place."

"I know you spend your mornings here. And a lot of afternoons and evenings. I thought I would surprise you. Surprise!"

Evelyn waved her hands in the air briefly. The faintest hint of a smile fluttered across Adam's lips. She decided to build on that.

"Do you want me to go kick that guy's ass? Because I will. I mean he's tall and all, but he's kind of skinny. I think I can take him. Especially if I hide somewhere and pop out at him."

"I have to go." Adam's light voice was barely audible.

"Go where?"

"Home."

"What, like…*home* home?" Evelyn's stomach clenched around the freezer waffles she'd had for breakfast.

Adam had never mentioned having to go back to whatever country he was from. He always said he wanted to focus on the moment and enjoy the time he had. She couldn't believe that time was up.

"When?"

"Three days."

"Three days!" She raised her hands, then slowly lowered them while she let out a deep breath. Bringing her voice to a more conversational volume, she said, "Wow. That's…soon."

"I requested an extension, but it was denied."

"Is that what that guy was telling you?"

"Yes."

"I guess this means the *Planet of the Apes* marathon is off. I can't see you wanting to spend ten of your remaining hours locked up in my apartment watching movies."

"That actually sounds wonderful."

Adam looked so sad. She probably mirrored his expression.

"Maybe we can go for a walk together first?" he asked.

A walk in the summer heat sounded awful, but being with him, helping him through this and spending every possible second with him overrode any complaints. She tried to smile, but only managed a nod.

"Sure."

They fell in step beside each other, walking close enough that their arms brushed. Adam caught her hand in his and entwined their fingers.

That was weird. He had always been stand-offish physically, only touching her to catch her if she stumbled on a trail or something.

What if this whole time he'd felt the same way about her as she did about him? What if she'd wasted moments they could have spent in each other's arms instead of watching sci-fi movies and eating popcorn on the couch?

If she looked at him she might start to cry, but she was dying to see his expression. She held her gaze steady on the ground. She wouldn't risk letting him see her cry. This was obviously hard enough on him as it was.

Evelyn tried to focus on his closeness. His hand dwarfed hers, his skin surprisingly smooth, given all his rock climbing and other adventurous pastimes. He had somehow persuaded her to come along on a few of them. She was in the best shape of her life thanks to their walks in this park, and they'd only explored a fraction of it. They wouldn't map every inch of it after all.

Her brain practically whirred as she tried to think of some way—any way—that they could have more time together. She wasn't ready for their relationship to be over.

She wasn't ready for him to leave.

"You could always put in for another visit, right?" she said.

"No. Where I'm from, they're very strict about where citizens can go. I was amazed they let me come here at all."

"Sounds like a pretty crappy place." Evelyn thought she murmured her sentiment quietly enough that he'd miss it, but his hearing was keener than that.

"I've never thought so before."

Before now, she finished for him. Not out loud, though.

"There are reasons behind the laws." Adam sounded more like he was trying to convince himself than her. "I understand why the limitations are in effect."

"Let me guess. You'd rather not explain them to me." She tried to smirk, to let him know she was joking, but her mouth wouldn't cooperate. It just kept pouring out smart-alecky comments—as usual.

"I'd rather enjoy the time I have left as much as possible. And I'd like to spend it with you."

Evelyn could set her own schedule since the professor supervising her PhD work was gone for the summer. The research journals she was supposed to be going through were piling up from the time she'd been spending with Adam, but she couldn't bring herself to care at the moment. Besides, she'd have plenty of time to catch up on them. As soon as Adam left.

This time, she managed to look up at him and conjure up a full—if fake—smile. "Whatever you want."

—

You can get your copy of **Gray Card** now! For more of my Paranormal Romances, check out **The Summer Park Psychics** or **Forbidden Instinct**. If you want to explore my other stories, you can go on out of this world adventures with the fated soulmates of the **Cygnian 7** series or check out short, steamy Sci-Fi Romances on a near-future Earth in that same universe with **The Department of Homeworld Security**. And if you'd like a little bit of Scifi mixed into your Paranormal Romance, check out the **Blades of Janus**.

I'd love to keep in touch. Join my newsletter at **cassandra-chandler.com/newsletter** to hear about all the adventures happening in Cassland. And if you enjoyed this book, please consider leaving a review at your favorite book review site. Reviews are so important to authors. You can also help by spreading the word among your friends. I appreciate you so much!

Thank you for reading *The Krampus!*

Cassandra Chandler

About the Author

USA Today Bestselling author Cassandra Chandler uses her vivid imagination to make the world more interesting, spawning the ideas she turns into her evocative Science Fiction Romances and enthralling Paranormal and Urban Fantasy Romances. Fast-paced and funny, lighthearted or tinged with shadow, her stories will introduce you to characters you'll fall in love with and worlds you long to explore.